Praise f...

These Fragile Graces, Th... ...

Kirkus Pick: Spring 2024 Top-10 SF Fantasy & Horror

"A queer anarchist commune in near-future Kansas City is threatened by corporate espionage in this fun and well-paced neo-noir cyberpunk adventure from Wasserstein (*All the Hometowns You Can't Stay Away From*). Theodora "Dora" Madsen lives in "self-imposed exile" from the commune she once called home, but when her ex-girlfriend, Kay, is found dead of an apparent overdose, Dora, suspicious, is compelled to investigate. Now an outsider to the tight-knit community, her investigations raise echoes of the conflict that led to her departure, and call into question the very principles on which the commune was founded. Can Dora discover the truth without tearing apart the community that sheltered her when she needed it most—and before someone else gets hurt? Wasserstein makes clever use of genre tropes, including clones, snappy noir-style dialogue, and the damaged, insomniac detective archetype. With a complex and enjoyably flawed trans protagonist and a portrayal of queer life that goes deeper than casual representation, this marks Wasserstein as a voice to watch out for in LGBTQ science fiction."

—*Publishers Weekly*

"With an anarchist's eye for flipping all the old tropes, Wasserstein makes her propulsive, stylish cyberpunk murder mystery sing on every page. Dora defines her own story, and it's absolutely engrossing."
—Karen Osborne, author of *Architects of Memory*

"This fast-paced novella blends a pitch-perfect noir voice with all the excitement and grit of an action movie, but at its core, it is ultimately a tale of community, identity, and connection. Izzy Wasserstein is a true and tender storyteller with a head for twisty plots and a heart for complex love."
—Emma Törzs, author of *Ink Blood Sister Scribe*

"Izzy Wasserstein has given us something we need, as only she can: a story about surviving the near-future hellscape that makes you want to survive the present hellscape. I know I'll be reading it again before long."
—Elly Bangs, author of *Unity*

"*These Fragile Graces, This Fugitive Heart* is an absorbing near future science-fiction novella that explores themes of identity and family with a keen eye for character and a central mystery that unfolds in unexpected ways. Izzy Wasserstein is a gifted writer, and this is a wonderful debut."
—Josh Rountree, author of *The Legend of Charlie Fish*

"This wise novella asks compelling questions about anarchism, community, self-determination, and consent, while allowing its trans and queer characters the full range of their flawed, messy humanity. Just like all of Izzy Wasserstein's work, this story is complex, well-written, and heartfelt."
—Natalia Theodoridou, World Fantasy Award winner and Nebula finalist

"[*These Fragile Graces*] does not give easy answers, but instead urges us to remember: the moment we lose sight of love—for our communities and for ourselves—is the moment we risk harming everything we hold dear."
—Naseem Jamnia, author of the Crawford-, Locus-, and World Fantasy–nominated novella *The Bruising of Qilwa*

"A fast-paced post-cyberpunk thriller that starts with a murder at an anarchist commune in Kansas City, and explores both the far-reaching and the intimately personal consequences. Read it, get immersed in the investigation, then find yourself thinking for a long while afterward."
—Bogi Takács, editor of *Transcendent 2: The Year's Best Transgender Speculative Fiction*

THESE FRAGILE GRACES, THIS FUGITIVE HEART

IZZY WASSERSTEIN

Also by Izzy Wasserstein

All the Hometowns You Can't Stay Away From (2022)

THESE FRAGILE GRACES

IZZY WASSERSTEIN

THIS FUGITIVE HEART

TACHYON
SAN FRANCISCO

Interior and cover design by Elizabeth Story
Author photo copyright © by Huascar Medina

Tachyon Publications LLC
1459 18th Street #139
San Francisco, CA 94107
415.285.5615
www.tachyonpublications.com
tachyon@tachyonpublications.com

Series editor: Jacob Weisman
Editor: Jaymee Goh

Print ISBN: 978-1-61696-412-2
Digital ISBN: 978-1-61696-413-9

Printed in the United States by Versa Press, Inc.

First Edition: 2024
9   8   7   6   5   4   3   2   1

For my trans family:
those who came before,
those still among us,
& those yet to come.

I HADN'T SEEN JUAN IN YEARS, not since I left the commune. When he showed up at my door, struggling to make eye contact, I knew that Kay was dead.

"Dora," he said, his hands flexing and releasing at his sides, as if trying to grasp something that wasn't there. "It's Kay."

An overdose, he explained. They'd found her this morning, unresponsive. I knew it was true, but I couldn't make sense of it. Not that she used. I knew that. Between illicit drugs and street-brewed versions of the corporate stuff, most people were on something. But she'd always been precise. Careful.

"I'm sorry to show up like this," Juan said into the silence. The yard's distance between us felt like much more. He'd been my closest friend, closer to me than anyone but Kay. Now neither of us knew where to look, where to put our hands. "I thought you should know, and I'd heard you live down here now—"

He was apologizing for telling me my ex was dead. Because I'd left, and he'd honored that. *Apologizing*. I felt ill.

"No!" I said, too forcefully. "No, Juan. Thank you. I'd have hated to find out . . ." I almost said "too late," my brain refusing to accept facts. Trailed off instead, then blurted out: "Can—can I see her?"

He flinched, then nodded. "Of course," he said. No one would be pleased that I was coming back, including me. I'd made damned sure of that when I left.

I'd sworn never to set foot in the commune again. Kept that vow for years and never thought I'd break it. Never thought I'd outlive Kay, either. I didn't want to face her body but couldn't do anything else.

Juan led me to the commune, past apartment buildings, "neighborhood" chain stores, and the occasional pawn shop and hole-in-the-wall restaurant, under the overpass that marked the line between very little wealth and none. Late October, and the heat made every step cost. When I'd last seen the old neighborhood, it had been lively. Elders at their windows or on stoops seeking relief from the heat, dealers on the corners, children playing wherever they could find shade. Things between the neighborhood and the commune were occasionally tense, sure, but there'd been a community here, people who knew one another, looked out for one another. And predators, like in any community. But a real neighborhood, in spite or because of poverty and oppression.

I'd missed this place. My current apartment was okay, best I could hope for, really. Reasonably safe, no big pest problems, even my own bathroom. But people in that neighborhood were clinging to the middle-class life their parents had. Something close to it, anyway. No one there looked out for one another. I'd never spoken to most of my neighbors. Kids didn't play in the streets. The desolation of the suburbs, recreated.

The old neighborhood had felt so alive. Now it was a ghost town. No one was out on the stoops, no faces in windows hoping for a breeze. One person on a corner bolted as soon as they saw us. The quiet put me on edge. Where had everyone gone?

The front of the commune was a patchwork of red brick and plywood. Two guards on the doorway—so the commune wasn't *entirely* ignoring security—were teens, maybe a decade younger than us. They looked at me with mild curiosity. The taller of the two said something in Tagalog and the other guard giggled and not-so-subtly shushed their comrade.

I was already one of the clueless older folks to them. When had that happened?

"Were we ever that young?" I asked Juan. His shoulders slumped; his eyes were caves.

"Not that long ago, Dora," he said. Don't think he believed it.

He knocked. A bolt clicked and the interior door opened. The common room was as I remembered it, once a restaurant for the rich, scarred and plastered over, furnished with scavenged and handmade tables and chairs. Seemed like the whole crew was there, clustered in small groups. At first, our arrival was greeted with vague interest. Then someone whispered my name, and tension rippled across the room. Someone I didn't know called their kid over, clutched them tight. Soon every eye followed me, some wary, a few angry, none pleased. I burn bridges.

I stopped myself from yanking up my hood, just pulled my shoulders back, gave a quick nod to Samara and Samuel, who at least weren't glaring, and followed Juan. I knew less than half the members, though I'd only been a few years in self-imposed exile. Through the kitchen, which smelled of yeast and sizzling vat protein, where more eyes stared, past what had been a courtyard and pool and was now the community garden, over to the personal rooms. Even before my memory implants, I couldn't have forgotten the way, but Juan led me. For my safety, or the community's? I didn't ask.

Up the stairs of the apartments that made up the rear of the commune. The hand-painted swirls on Kay's door were peeling like a tired metaphor. Juan put his hand on the latch, looked back at me.

"You ready?" he asked, more gently than I deserved.

"Not sure. But I'm doing it anyway." Some things you've got to see, ready or not.

Sun sliced between the boards covering the wide window, thoughtless of its bright cruelty. Kay lay on her back. Someone had closed her eyes, wiped the vomit from her lips, mopped it up from the sheet as best they could, and put her on her back. Her brown skin was ashen. Can't say she looked peaceful, but she was past hurting. I stared, even though I knew this sight would stay with me forever. I'd barely functioned before the memory enhancement, but the tech has a cost: I don't forget, not even when I want to. I knew I'd never escape this last memory of her.

Maybe you only find a love like her once in your life. Who's to say if that's a curse or a blessing?

"She was always so careful," I said. Careful about drugs, not about the commune. I'd told myself that's why we'd split. Don't think I ever really believed it.

"Careful isn't always enough," Juan said. As if I didn't know.

I made myself lean close. Didn't care that she was cold. I pressed my lips to her forehead, meaning it as our parting. It wasn't enough. Tears weren't coming, so I pulled her against me, mirroring the last hug she'd given me before I left. She'd always felt dangerously thin, one of many reasons I'd feared for her safety, even at those times when I hadn't given a shit about my own. Even now I wanted to worry.

When I'd stormed out of the commune, cursing them for fools, all grief and anger and wounded pride, I told myself I was over her. Now I clutched her body like it would do any good. My hands clawed. The points of her shoulder blades were sharp under her worn shirt. Between them . . . something.

Carefully I turned her over, pulled down the shirt. No way anyone would have noticed the needle's puncture if it weren't for the bump around it, red and swollen, as clear an allergic reaction as you could ask for.

"Who found her body?" I snapped.

Juan stopped giving me space, came up to look for himself.

"Oh shit," he said.

I asked again. Sharper.

"Ly. Lylah. When Kay didn't come down for breakfast."

"Tell me someone saved the syringe, Juan."

Someone had. It was set in a box by the corner, next to the rag they'd used to clean up, waiting for safer disposal. I tore a corner from Kay's corkboard. My contributions, a couple sketches of us, some bad poetry, and a tattoo design, had been purged long ago, replaced with mementos of other loves. I corked the syringe's tip, carefully wrapped the whole thing and stuck it in my messenger bag. Pulled out my .38, confirmed it was loaded, and clipped it to my belt.

"The gun, Dora, really?" Juan asked, eyes wide. It wouldn't win me friends in the commune, but I didn't give a single shit.

"Someone here killed her," I said. I could see he didn't want to believe that, his eyes moving between me and Kay's body. But he knew it, too.

"Fuck," he said. Our nightmares come to life. Kay killed, and it would be easy for this to tear the community apart.

Well. I've always been better in a crisis.

"Gather them up," I said. "Everyone. I'm solving this."

I'm no PI, but I've seen my share. Since I left the commune, I'd survived by selling my skill in operational security. I hadn't set foot in the commune in years, which meant I was the only one who wasn't a suspect.

"Are you sure you're the right person for this, Dora?" Juan asked. As close as we'd been, now he didn't want to say the obvious. They'd hate me for this.

"Who else?" I let him do the math. No one here, not the cops, who only came to the ghetto in force, and only then when the rich folks who ran the show demanded it. Not some PI the commune couldn't afford. Me or no one.

"I'll ask them," he said. "You know I can't make anyone agree." Good luck making a few dozen anarchists agree on much of anything.

"Convince them. Remind them what it will look like if they refuse."

He stared at me like I was a stranger. Or a fucking cop. When he left, I searched the room. Nothing more to see, just Kay murdered.

"I'll find them, Kay," I told her. As if that would fix anything. My specialty is breaking things.

The worry and hatred in people's eyes had been replaced by fear. Furtive glances, shifting weight, hands clenching and unclenching. Everyone processing what it meant that someone who called the KC Commune their home had done this. They'd shared labor, meals, a roof, a dream with someone who had killed Kay. It's one thing for a crime of passion. Horrible, but understandable. But premeditated, covered up? A disaster so big they were willing to tolerate me.

I started with Lylah, whose name featured prominently on Kay's corkboard. The new girl-friend, cis but still looking too much like me. Lylah was white with deep-set eyes, sharp nose, jaw jutting against the world.

I'd called her into what passed for the security office, a couple square yards of space, the feed from a solar-powered camera covering the street out-side the front door, a handful of weapons. About as much privacy as I could get. I wanted to ask Juan to interview others, give people less time to sort out their stories. But I wouldn't put that on him or any-one else. "I've got nothing to say to you," she said.

"You were her girlfriend."

"Your point?"

"You need me to solve this."

"Like hell do I need anything from you."

"The partner's the most likely suspect," I said.

"Or the ex." That hatred in her eyes: because I'd hurt Kay? Or because I'd loved her?

"If you're innocent, I'm your best hope of prov-ing it." I tried to soften my tone. For all the good it did.

"Juan's a fool to trust you," she said. I met her eyes, neither of us flinching.

"You'd best start thinking about who you can trust," I said, figuring it was worth a shot. "And about what happens to Kay's dream if we don't solve this." No one had believed in the commune, in what it was and what it could be, more than Kay.

"We," Lylah spat.

I tried the twins next, since their gaze didn't cut.

"Strange? I mean, Kay had been quiet lately." Samara anticipated my next question. "For the last month or so. Not a lot to say in meetings, just kind of distant."

"Were you worried about her?" I asked. The twins exchanged looks. They were so alike. Same pointed chins, same cheekbones like ancient statuary. Until Samuel had started T, no one could tell them apart. Now he had a neatly-cropped beard, and a jagged scar, bone-white against his olive skin, ran down his left cheek. A tightness filled my gut. This world had moved on without me.

"Not really?" Samuel said, or asked.

"Or only in retrospect," Samara added. Her twin nodded. They were in accord. "You know how it is. People looked up to Kay. Lots was on her shoulders. I don't think it would have been remarkable, except . . ."

She trailed off. I let it linger, that old interview trick, but she didn't, maybe couldn't, finish the thought.

"Who was upset with her?" I asked. "Or might have wished her harm?"

"This kind of harm? I can't imagine," Samuel said. Stared at his boots. "You know Kay. She's impossible not to like."

True. I'd come to the commune as a desperate street kid, fleeing an abusive home. I'd learned lots about surviving, but I'm not sure how much longer I'd have lasted if they hadn't taken me in. The community saved my life, and I'd loved it immediately, and Kay almost as quickly.

But there was something the twins weren't saying. Old friends, and I thought they still liked me. But if there was one thing everyone in the commune agreed upon, it was *don't be a fucking narc.*

So I pressed them, and got some answers. There was tension, even between Kay and Juan, a split within the commune about how much to engage with what remained of the neighborhood. Things were worse than ever out there: few jobs, no money, no interest from what passed for city government, which mostly just paid cops and kept the lights on in the better neighborhoods. The slow-burn governmental collapse of my childhood had become an inferno in the years before I found the commune, the years when I was on the street, behind bars. Chaos at every level. The city was barely hanging on. Last I heard there was officially a state government, but that was mostly a fiction. Militias and the occasional sheriff ran things in rural areas. As for the feds, who knew what they were doing? Presumably trying to hold on to what power they had, hold off threats foreign and domestic. The shit governments do, only now without the pretense of being for everyone.

Other powers emerged in the vacuum. Corporations bought or claimed public utilities, raised their own police forces, and generally proved as hearty as ticks. Fascist militias are always eager to step in when people are afraid. Churches, gangs, and utopians, everyone scrambled for what was left. Used to be the big powers in the commune's neighborhood were gangs. But that had changed since I left. There wasn't even much gang presence, which was good in some ways, but also meant there was no one offering any kind of security. Those folks who had stuck around were on their own. People had been leaving, especially over the last year, so things had grown worse as everyone lost their neighbors, friends, the connections that had offered some safety. Kay had wanted to do more to help. Of course. Others wanted to stick with their chosen family, leave those outside the commune to make their own choices. An old argument, too much like the one that had been my last straw, but this one hadn't been angry, without even much shouting, and at the commune shouting was common as summer sunburns.

"Who was Kay's dealer?" I asked.

"No one in the commune," Samara said. "Someone from the neighborhood. I don't know who."

"What about Lylah? What was their relationship like?"

The twins' eyes narrowed, and again their gazes met.

"I don't like asking," I told them. "But I have to."

"They ran hot and cold," Samuel said after a long moment. "Not like you think. They never even raised their voices at each other, not that I heard."

"It was hard to keep track of when they were

together or separated," Samara added.

"That can get ugly quick." I hated being compared to a cop, hated acting like one even more, but I needed answers, even if people loathed the questions. If being hated was the price of solving Kay's murder, I'd pay it.

"I just can't see Lylah doing something like that," Samara said.

"But I can't see anyone here doing it," Samuel added. "What kind of monster . . . I can't think like that. I won't."

It was all I could think about.

"Keep an eye out, will you?" I asked the twins. "Whoever did this will feel the strain. Act weird." Unless they wouldn't feel it. Unless they were a predator in a mask of mutual aid. That had happened before, and one of our own had been killed, a friend of mine. I felt responsible for Fix's death, warned them it would happen again. I'd burned every bridge to try to make them see. And for what? Kay was dead. Nausea twisted my guts.

Next up was Valk. She was a few years younger than me and had been new to the commune when I left. I barely knew her. Juan said she was Kay's best friend. That made her a potential witness.

Or suspect. She fought ineffectually against tears, one of those white girls whose genetics left veins visible beneath achingly pale skin, who weren't meant for the six-month summers of Kansas City. Not that things were much better up north, from what I heard. Probably there was someplace that wasn't burning or flooding or otherwise hollowed out by climate change, but I'd never heard where. Looking at Valk made me grateful for my mom's Sephardic heritage, the relative darkness of my skin.

Like the others, Valk hadn't seen anything unusual on the night of. The whole commune, packed into an old hotel, and no one had seen shit.

"Who might want to harm Kay?"

"Everyone loved her," Valk managed over hiccups. "You were friends, right?" She wiped her nose on her sleeve. "Sorry. I just—she always saw the best in people. How could anyone hate someone who looked out for everyone?"

Even after I left, I'm sure Kay didn't hate me. Pretty sure.

"Someone hated her enough to kill her," I said, and Valk choked off another sob.

"No one here would kill her," she said. "I won't believe that."

"Then who would?" I left aside the question of how a stranger could have moved through the whole commune, snuck into Kay's room, killed her, and staged the scene.

Valk hesitated, eyes shifting back and forth as though we were being spied on, even though the room had no camera, no equipment, just a screen with the feed from the commune's single security camera that faced only the exterior street. It was there for the cops or the militias who might look for trouble. No surveillance of members of the commune. Everyone agreed on that. Valk swallowed hard and leaned in.

My phone chirped. On reflex, I pulled a pill from my bag, dry-swallowed it.

"ARS?" she asked, wiping at her eyes. "Sorry, don't mean to pry. My mom has it."

Lots of people experienced the joy of suppressing their immune response to early-gen body mods. Some decided dealing with Augment Rejection Syndrome wasn't worth the trouble and had their enhancements removed. Others wouldn't or couldn't. I was in both camps, needing my memory implants to function and not having any safe way to remove them, so I got the pleasure of scraping together funds to keep myself on expensive corporate medication and prayed someone would make a viable street version soon. A friend of mine was working on exactly that.

Didn't mean I planned to commiserate about it.

"I was an early adopter," I said. "You were saying?"

But the interruption had fucked up the moment. She was skittish as those invasive wall lizards, darting everywhere, swarming in the heat.

"Nothing," she said, "it's nothing."

"I need your help, Valk. Please."

Dead Gods help her if she ever faced a real interrogation. I'd rarely met anyone easier to read. She was terrified, at risk of a panic attack. Her lip trembled, and she leaned in again.

"In the neighborhood," she whispered, her mouth a centimeter from my ear. "They talk about a company. BioJesus."

"Bio-Jesus?" I asked, incredulous. No way anyone else could have heard me, but she cringed.

"Gesis," she said. "G-E-S-I-S."

"What about them?"

But she'd said all she dared, just looked at me, gray-eyed and hopeless. "I don't know. But I'm scared, Dora."

Fear was a luxury I couldn't afford. Anger was cheaper.

I didn't hear about BioGesis again from any of the others, didn't ask about it. A false lead can poison the well. Closing a case without caring much if you've got the right perp might work for cops, but I wanted justice. Or revenge. Take your pick. No one expressed concerns about security, either, which I guess was a comfort. Quieted the voices that said she'd still be alive if I'd fought harder, made my case better. If I'd protected her. If I'd stayed.

As if proving it wasn't my fault would make her any less dead. Pathetic, Dora.

Kay's dealer had a first name, Herc. No last name that anyone knew. He hadn't been seen around lately. Like most everyone on these blocks. From what I heard it was just the commune and some elders, ancient and stubborn as the weeds that tore up concrete.

No one could say for sure who was the last person to see Kay alive. I figured Lylah for it, but no one had seen her go into or leave Kay's room before finding the body, and they didn't spend nights together. I'm not proud of it, but that made me feel a bit better, like there was some space that was only for me. What a fool.

I saved Juan for last. He didn't know anything new.

"Watch everyone," I said. "Whoever did this will tip their hand." Pretty sure I kept my own doubts off my face.

"Paranoia is the last thing we need, Dora," he said. I could feel it already, the way this investigation would break whatever ties held our friendship together.

"Last thing we need is another body turning up," I said.

"Don't let your revenge—"

"It's not that—"

"—Whatever. Reckoning. Don't let it tear down what we've grown here."

"Don't care about the commune more than the people in it." My words were sharper than I'd intended. Probably his had been, too. Would've been better if we'd just slapped each other.

"Fuck you, Dora," Juan said. We glared for a long moment. Then he left. Nothing more to say.

On my way out, I pulled up my hoodie, stuffed my hands in my pockets so no one would see them shaking. I had a long walk ahead, and needed it to steady myself.

▼

The city wasn't safe. City cops weren't even pretending to protect and serve, at least not in the neighborhoods people like me were welcome in. Some places had rent-a-cops or contracted corporate muscle when they needed it, but unless you had the kind of money that let you live in some high-walled enclave, or had value to someone with that kind of money, your safety came down to you and the people who looked out for you. Same as ever, for the poor, the dark-skinned, the disabled.

Didn't mean it was some hellscape out of an old vid. If you walked with purpose, stayed alert, and knew the neighborhoods, you were usually okay. I headed down Main, past the toppled light-rail car, weeds growing through its shattered windows. Up on the hills, rich folks' homes gleamed in the sun. They'd lived down here once, and you could see where the money had gone, before the floods, the droughts, the wilting of the government out east. Before the richer-than-rich all left and the merely rich sealed themselves away in exurban strongholds or corporate enclaves.

I'd been raised middle-class, which in KC meant the suburbs, back when there'd been real suburbs, back when there'd been a bit more middle. Maybe there was still something like that, somewhere. Not in downtown KC. Not anywhere I'd ever been. When the university closed, my father managed to find work as a government contractor. Putting to use that series of fancy, obsolete letters after his name (MD, PhD, DPhil, probably more I'm forgetting). Don't know what they wanted with a specialist in neurocognition. Hoping to make a weapon, I suppose. So he got paid, which I guess made us lucky. But he was also the bastard who chased my mom away, whose greatest pleasure in life was telling me all the ways I'd disappointed him, who found my dresses and burned them in front of me, so you could say I didn't feel lucky. Ran away for the first time at thirteen and kept running until it stuck.

That wasn't a lot more than a decade ago, yet it felt impossibly far away. There'd been some public schools still, then, and if you turned on the tap or flicked a light switch, mostly you could expect water or power. Lots of people desperate to save a patient who was already dead.

Q: How does a nation die?

A: Slowly, then all at once.

Back in the day they'd talk about late-stage capitalism. A cancer killing the human species, the planet. But cancer dies with its host. Probably the capitalists were already on their way to another planet, or a deep-sea city. They're betting the disease is terminal for us. Not for them.

I almost wish I could be there when they learn better.

I was hiding from my thoughts, not ready to deal with Kay's loss. Keeping busy. I was good at that.

Styles's neighborhood was an old one. First it had been manufacturing, then housing for the young and wealthy. Now those units were divided into tiny residences, a quiet neighborhood where rent wasn't entirely out of most people's reach and electricity and city water could be had for the right price. People here were doing okay. For now. Maybe the very rich or very delusional thought even this center could hold. Everyone else was waiting for the next punch. The storm that would wipe away the city. The next drought, even worse than the last one. Bioweapons or just plain old disease, old-fashioned war or nukes.

But we were still hanging on. For now.

Styles lived in an old redbrick. They buzzed me up right away, let me into their cramped studio, a furrow cut across their brow.

"What's up, Dora?" they asked. They trusted me, let me up with no questions asked. I didn't have lots of friends, but Styles and I were close. I'd run security for one of their parties not long after I left the commune. Needed the job desperately, and I think Styles knew it. Ended up being a huge success. I had the pleasure of beating the shit out of a dude with a 1488 tattoo and a sawed-off shotgun. Styles paid me double and even hooked me up with estrogen implants. That had been a good night.

"I need your expertise," I said, and they offered me a seat on the only chair. They sat down on their bed, pulled the sweep of their hair back and pinned it, the way they always did when they were going to work through a problem.

"Fill me in," they said. I cued up some thumping stas-core on my phone, let it play as I leaned in, pulled out the syringe.

"Someone turned up dead," I said. "And whatever was in here is the reason why." I gave them the details that mattered, keeping Kay's name off my lips. Wish I could say I was thinking about security best practices, but I just couldn't make myself explain.

"I'll see what I can figure out," Styles said. They did biochem work, way beyond me, for some Big Ag outfit promising to "reclaim the plains" from desert. They could afford much more than this room with its one high window, but spent what they had on parties and distribution of gray-market meds. I'm pretty sure they did that at a loss. Styles was good people.

"I owe you," I said.

They opened their mouth, closed it again. "Consider it a deposit on your next contract," they said, kind enough to offer me a transaction instead of a favor. The lack of personal obligation seemed easier, somehow. Ever since I left the commune. Even with Styles.

"Done," I said.

"This is urgent, yeah?"

I nodded. "Yeah. I've got a bad feeling . . ."

Styles grimaced. "Got it. I'll ping you when I know something."

"Sec—"

"Securely, of course." They laughed. "I have

learned *something* from you, Dora. I'll use the protocol."

Dusk gathered as I walked home, freeing me from the need to duck from shadow to shadow, but still hot enough that the breeze plastered my shirt to my body. Kay's face kept slipping into my thoughts, that murdered face, and each time I made myself go further back and remember her smile. A migraine built behind my right eye.

I walked down streets I knew well, past a bar whose security system I'd set up, across from an old warehouse now serving as a community daycare. I was lost in the past. A great way to get jumped.

I heard them coming just before the blow landed, flinched away as everything exploded to stars. I hit the pavement, rolled over. My attacker was already on top of me. About my size, hooded, grabbing at my throat. I brought my arms up and out, knocking theirs away. They threw punches, hard, wild, angry. Personal, then.

Shielded my face best I could, and when they drew back for a harder blow, I jammed my palm into their sternum. They rocked back and I rolled hard, pitching them off. I scrambled atop them, pulled my hand back—

The hood had fallen away, and they had my face.

Well, no. My face through a funhouse mirror, if I'd never started estrogen, never blocked T. Sharp lines, even sharper than mine, a beard as neatly trimmed as any mansion's lawn. And those muddy brown eyes. I thought I'd seen hatred before. Nothing like this.

I hesitated. His?—fuck, I guess?—cross clipped my ear, then he twisted, tipped me off him. The world tilted as I struggled to my feet. He was already up, fumbling in his pocket, reaching for what had to be a gun. I stumbled at him, nothing but unsteady momentum. We impacted and tumbled back to the ground, blood dripping off my face, disappearing onto his black clothes. Both of us dazed, but I knew something crucial. He could have shot me in the back of the head, but he'd wanted the personal violence instead. Big mistake. It's not as easy to kill someone as most people think.

He kept digging for his weapon, so I hammered against his temple. Dazed and bleeding, he still managed to draw the handgun, tried to level it. I grabbed his wrist. Couldn't match his strength, didn't have to. His free hand flailed at me without much impact. All rage, no training, no focus. I twisted, slammed his arm to the ground. His gun slid away.

I was off-balance. He threw me aside, rushed for the gun. Another mistake. I pulled mine, screamed a warning.

"I'll shoot!"

He was crouched, halfway to his weapon, neither surrendering nor grabbing for it. I pulled myself to my feet. Self-preservation's a strong impulse. Most people back down in a situation like that. But when I edged around to where I could see both his hands and his face, his teeth were bared, his gaze like looking down two barrels. Motherfucker wanted me dead.

"Doesn't have to be this way," I said. "You can still walk away. Don't make me end you."

He hesitated, took several breaths. I let him see I wasn't kidding.

"You *abomination*," he bellowed, and lunged for his weapon.

I fired. Tried to incapacitate him, but shooting to injure isn't like people think. The bullet caught him in the face. Blood and bone splattered against my hands, my cheeks. He dropped, twitching. Then went still.

No shakes yet. Those would come later. I looked both ways down the alley. If anyone had seen, they'd made themselves scarce. Patted down the corpse. No ID, no phone, not even a card with a pittance of crypto. Just a dead man who'd had my old face. Until he didn't.

I grabbed his 9mm and left him where he lay. This wasn't a neighborhood the cops gave two shits about, and no rent-a-cop was going to make a John Doe their business. Best thing I could do was get clear.

I'd hoped to make it home before the shakes started. Got halfway.

Made it to my place just in time to empty my stomach contents into the toilet, then sagged to the cool bathroom tile. My fan dried the sweat on my face to salt crystals. It's not that I've left lots of bodies. Never killed anyone who wasn't determined to kill someone else, or me. Even those stay with you.

I rolled onto my back, burned through an expensive chunk of data researching BioGesis. A newer player, selling themselves as "a leader in biological research and human life extension." Looked to be well funded. Unusual for KC, when so much money and power had migrated north. That suggested they either lacked the resources to play with the big corps or were hoping to avoid scrutiny.

They had a big shining building up where the university hospital used to be, the kind of place where I'd never get in the door. Didn't make sense that they'd care about squatters in boarded-up downtown apartments.

I thought I'd fall asleep there, the tile heating under me, but that grotesque face kept floating before me, and then Kay's, enough to make me wish for the days when I could still forget, when dissociation had kept me alive. Probably for the best that I couldn't recall too many details of my parents' screaming matches, of my father's attempts to make me be a boy, of those first years on the street when what remained of the safety net snapped, when disease and hunger stepped into the vacuum of the failed state, before a hand-ful of corporations had claimed what they wanted and left the rest to be picked over like carrion. Not all bad, the holes in my pre-implant memory. But like a lot of defense mechanisms, it carried costs. Waking nightmares could bleed into sleep, so I forced myself up and drank three glasses of water from the rain harvester on the fire escape outside my window. My filter was due for re-placement, but I couldn't afford it. Had to take my chances, like with everything else. Jobs had been hard to come by. Rent and meds took most of what I made. And things would get worse, since there was no way I'd be taking any new work right now. Only thing that mattered was solving Kay's murder. I spent my week's water allowance on a shower. Couldn't swear I got all of my attacker out of my hair, but I felt a little like a person again.

If I couldn't sleep, I'd work. I popped a stim, dressed, reloaded my revolver, tucked the 9mm beneath my mattress, and headed back to my old neighborhood. The western wind was a whip, blessedly cool air rushing ahead of a front. With any luck, a storm was coming.

My neighborhood still had a handful of work-ing streetlights, some civic-minded residents having wired them to solar panels, but by the time I passed under the interstate I'd crossed the border from "poor" to "destitute"; from neigh-borhoods where some people still had jobs and hopes of doing a little better, to ones where the most desperate had been left to live or die on their own. On that side of the highway, the only light came from up the hill and reflected off the low clouds, so buildings and people became gray ghosts in the night.

A hint of movement. I tensed. Just someone sleeping against a pillar, their ancient phone pinging a request for help. I'd been there, battered by the elements, by angry hands. There'd been nights when a stranger's generosity had saved my life. I didn't have much, but much wasn't nothing. I transferred a bit their way. They stirred, mut-tered a thanks.

The rain came, thick sheets of it in the wind. The pavement hissed like a griddle. No streetlights in my old neighborhood, everything boarded up, the commune and the old apartments, the abandoned church down the street, and not even a flicker of candlelight or hijacked electric light. A dead neighborhood, now, just me, the steam rising from manholes, and puddles throwing muddy light back to the sky.

I wasn't looking for anything in particular, only sorting thoughts, trying to regain my sense of the place. Maybe get a sense of who was still hanging on here. Then two figures rose out of the darkness in front of me, sheltering under an overhang, dark shadows in the gray black. Too far away for me to recognize them, but this had to be about the commune. The neighborhood was all but deserted, and no one would meet in the middle of the night unless they were eager to avoid attention. And right after Kay's murder? No way it was a coincidence. I pressed against a wall and watched. The shorter one gestured broadly, the taller barely moved. Then they parted, the short one heading away from me, up the street towards the commune. The other watched them for a long moment, then stuffed their hands in their pockets and walked towards me. I ducked around the corner, let them pass, then followed for a few blocks. They turned down an alleyway, where they'd parked an honest-to-Gods car. High-end, too, with treads that could handle the collapsing, pothole-strewed streets. How long it had been since anyone had driven a car in this neighborhood? I drew my gun, closed the distance. They tensed just as I reached them, put their hands in the air.

"I don't carry money, and the auto's biolocked," they said, deep-voiced and steady. Like having a loaded gun staring them down was just the cost of doing business.

"I'm not here to rob you," I said. Rain spattered off my hood. "Turn around."

They did, for all the good it did me. Long black coat, wide-brimmed hat, like a character from an old vid. A pale face, smooth, their irises ringed with light.

"Who were you talking to back there?"

They tilted their head. "Let's be civilized. You can call me Mr. Smith. And you are?"

"Answer the question, Mr. Smith."

"I'll answer for you, then. You're Theodora Madsen," Smith said. I'd seen those eyes, seen the car, wasn't shocked. Smith probably had full data privileges on a satellite relay. He was analyzing my data in real time. Couldn't imagine what that cost.

"You'd be wise not to fuck with me," I said,

and tugged at the only thread I had. "I'll ask you once more. Who were you talking to?"

"I can't tell you," he said. "I think you know that."

"I've had a very bad day, Mr. Smith." I pressed my thumb to the hammer. With his enhanced vision, there'd be no mistaking the motion. "You're going to give me answers."

"Not as many as you'd like." His hands hadn't moved. "I have professional obligations, Ms. Madsen."

I hated that surname, never used it. Hated how it tied me to biology, to my asshole father, who'd chased off my mother and tried to force me to stay. Hated that Smith could pull it from some database and inflict it on me. At least he had my real first name. More or less.

"I'm sure. So I could just shoot you, then see who comes sniffing around."

He stared at me, two rings of light and an untroubled face. "You could. And I can't stop you. Are your questions worth killing for?"

He'd called my bluff. I wasn't going to shoot him if I didn't have to. If I knew he was involved in Kay's death, maybe that would have been enough to break my rule against cold-blooded killing. Maybe. Colder than cold, this one. I tried something new.

"What does your employer want with this place?" I demanded. Took a chance. "What's Bio-Gesis's interest here?"

He scoffed. "I'm not with BioGesis, Ms. Madsen. I think we have a common interest. We both want to find out what BioGesis is up to."

"Then we should share info," I said, almost daring him.

"I'm not authorized to do that," Smith said.

"Then get authorized. If we really have common cause, then this is how you prove it."

After a few moments' silence, he inclined his head.

"No promises. I'll consult with my employer. All I can say for now is that if you want answers, keep digging into BioGesis."

I sensed that was all I was going to get from him. I lowered my gun. Slightly. "Go on, then," I said, and Smith went.

I stared into the darkness for long minutes after he left. Nothing but the rain and memories. Old ones, fragmented and rotting: my mother's face, with laugh lines, though I rarely heard her laugh. My father's, imperious and oh-so-disappointed.

And new ones, stored with precision by my memory augment: that uncanny not-quite-me, his face exploding. Kay's, most cruelly of all, in the moment of climax.

And some people say ghosts aren't real.

The commune had bolt-holes for emergencies. But anyone using them to sneak back in would be noticed. They'd more likely use the front door, where any member could come and go as they liked. I knew it as well as anyone. It was part of why I'd broken with the community. The consensus had been that the principles of voluntary association outweighed my security concerns. I'd argued that some impositions were necessary to stop further violence. I hadn't said it calmly. Lost that argument, and you might say I didn't take it well.

They had a guard posted, though, who shouted "Who goes?" before I'd even seen them. I put my hands up, approached. Lylah.

"You," she said.

"Me. Lylah, did someone just come this way?"

She raised an eyebrow.

"It's urgent," I said, though the smaller figure could have been her.

"I'm not going to snitch, you fucking cop."

"I'm not . . ." I forced myself to tamp down my fury. Lack of sleep and too much horror for one day had frayed me. This was about Kay, not me. "Someone's conspiring against the commune, and they just came this way," I said. "Good money that whoever it is killed Kay." Couldn't be sure of that, but two people meeting in an abandoned neighborhood after a murder, and one of them came this way? Too big to be a coincidence.

Lylah hesitated, the grimace of someone at war with herself. Maybe if I hadn't been an outsider. Or hadn't been Kay's ex. She stayed silent.

"If it was you, I'll find out." I couldn't resist the provocation.

"Get the fuck out of here." She spat at my feet.

"You can't turn me away without the community's support," I said. "Unless the community agreements have changed." I was pretty sure they hadn't. I wasn't a fascist, an enemy, or a cop, no matter what Lylah might think. There'd been no vote to cast me out. Nothing to stop me from seeking shelter. I'd given a diatribe against those rules and felt almost no shame in making use of them.

Even in the barely-there light, she looked angry enough to kill. I didn't see a weapon. Didn't mean much. Maybe she had one. Maybe she'd shoot me if I turned my back. We stared, hating each other for who we were and who we might be.

"I'm taking an empty room for the night." I turned my back to her, headed inside, and didn't eat a bullet. First thing that had gone right all day.

There was no one in the security room. I played back the recorded feed, but it was old tech, and darkness and rain meant I couldn't even make out my own approach.

I took one of the empty rooms, pulled a stop from my bag and wedged it under the door. Unsatisfied, I shoved the mattress against it and collapsed, my back to the door. The mattress was only a couple inches thick and smelled of mildew, but it was dry. I pulled it around me like a tortilla, slipped in and out of sleep.

No one came for me in the night. I ate breakfast at the commune, putting my back to the wall and watching. Eyes slid over me like oil, everyone wanting to pretend I wasn't there, wanting even more to keep an eye on me. Protein porridge was no better than I remembered it, but still I was testing their generosity, the spirit that said they would care for an outsider unless given good reason not to. I was testing the limits of that commitment. The prodigal daughter returned, but not welcome. What would my father say to that comparison?

Look at you, Theodore. So grandiose, even in your self-pity. So much from those days was gone, lost to the fog of trauma and time. But his reproachful voice? Clearer than clear.

The commune's chatter was subdued. No surprise there. I didn't learn anything from it. Only the young children chasing one another in circles cut the mood. If you weren't careful, you'd confuse their laughter for screams.

Samara and Samuel entered, mixed some garden greens with the best vat-grown protein, fresh from the basement. Only hesitated a moment before joining me. A kindness. They were the first friendly faces I'd seen. The commune had no set schedule. I hadn't seen Juan, and feared how he might look at me.

"You were right," I said, "the neighborhood's different. Almost deserted."

"There are a few folks left." Samara picked at her food. "But lots have cleared out."

"Any idea why?"

She paused, dropped her voice to barely more than a whisper. "I heard a rumor that someone was paying them to leave."

That didn't make sense. Decades ago, this neighborhood had been part of some downtown revitalization plan, had been desirable, drawing mostly young, white folks with money. Pushing out everyone else. But those times were long past, those gentrifiers off to somewhere else. Up north, or the exurbs, or who knew where. There was nothing here anymore that money noticed.

"Who'd bother with that?"

"Right?" she said. "It doesn't make sense. Anyway, it's just a rumor. Not even one from a source I trust."

"We used to know this neighborhood," Samuel said. "Even our enemies. We knew where we stood."

"We?" I asked.

"The two of us, the commune, anyone paying attention. It was messy, but it was a neighborhood. People who knew each other, trying to survive. Even if they were enemies, there was—something. A shared experience. Not just a bunch of buildings."

"Now there aren't many faces, and mostly we don't know them," Samara added. I thought of what I'd seen last night, kept it to myself. Couldn't see the twins as killers, but couldn't buy a stim tab for what that was worth.

"You get any corporate interest down here?" I asked instead.

They stared at me, incredulous.

"Here?" Samara asked.

"Not in our lifetimes," Samuel said.

When I didn't have more to ask, he went on. "How are you, Dora? How's life?" Seemed like he meant it. He'd always had the better posture between them, one of the few ways to tell them apart, back in the day, but now his shoulders were slumped as far down as his sister's. Her dark eyes were in constant motion, scanning my face, while his were fixed, crinkled with concern. They were worried about me. Kay's face rose in my mind's eye, dead and sorrowful.

"Hanging on," I said.

We caught up a little. I figured they'd talked, decided my ugly departure from the commune, complete with my self-immolating breakup with Kay, didn't mean we weren't still friends. Friendly. Something. When they headed to a shift cleaning the air filters, I stood to leave. All eyes turned to me, then away. Only one pair watched longer. Valk, raccoon-eyed, jittery as cornered prey. Like me, she'd pressed her back to the wall. If she suspected BioGesis, why did she act like a killing blow might come from someone in the commune?

Or maybe it was me she feared. Couldn't blame her.

The sky was the color of corrupted memory. My hair plastered to my neck, the storm's brief respite gone with the sunrise, the air swamp-thick, summer-hot. I needed to get my sense of the neighborhood back. What remained of the neighborhood. A femme on one corner ghosted the moment they saw me. The dealer two corners down tensed but sold me a couple stim tabs. I asked if they'd seen Herc, but got nothing out of it, except the lines in their face drawn even tighter. I ducked beneath an overhang a block down. In an hour of watching, I didn't see anyone come through who wasn't buying, didn't see a single face I recognized.

Afternoon poured heat into air you could nearly swim through.

I wandered for blocks in each direction, looking for Herc, or someone who knew where I could find him. Even a friendly face. I didn't have to go far to find busier blocks, locals hanging on as best they could. But these weren't areas I knew well, which made them dangerous. People on the stoops didn't know me and unfamiliar crews ran the corners.

Whatever was driving the exodus, it was limited to a few square blocks. What did those who'd left know that the commune didn't?

Took me hours before I saw a face I knew. Everybody called him Zeke. He'd been on the outskirts of one of the gangs, a runner and spotter. Smalltime. Maybe he'd seen something useful.

"It's cool," Zeke said as I approached, keeping his hands in sight, his eyes scanning the area before settling on me. He'd curled up against an effaced stone figure, centerpiece of a long-dry fountain, tucked into its shadow while it lasted. "I've been waiting for you, see?"

I had no idea what he was talking about. I stopped two yards from him, let him take my silence as he would.

"It's true," Zeke said, scratching at a bare arm. "Think I'd be out here if I wanted trouble? Tell your boss I'll take the deal."

"What were you offered?" I asked, knowing each word might tip him off that I wasn't working for whoever he thought I was.

He looked at me strangely, told me a number. A pittance, even in this neighborhood. If this was payment for leaving, it was a very small carrot. Watching him try to mask fear, I could imagine the stick.

"I'm not with . . ." I let Zeke draw his own conclusions.

"Shit. Shit. I don't want any trouble," he said again. "Look, I'm trying to play nice here." He retreated, limping towards an alleyway, one leg visibly swollen.

"One more thing," I called after him. He flinched but turned to face me. I came up to him, transferred him some funds from my rapidly disappearing savings. Not much, but enough to soften the lines in his face.

"Which corner is Herc's these days?" I asked.

He gawked at me like I'd grown several new appendages.

"Herc's gone. Long gone." His laugh bordered on full-blown panic. "Anyway, uh, thanks." I could see clear as day: he was terrified to refuse me, terrified to be seen with me.

For the second time in two days I got jumped like an amateur. I'd set my usual string on my place's door frame, and it was undisturbed. Didn't think twice before I stepped inside, right up until I felt the crack to the back of my skull. Everything went white. Next thing I knew I was on the floor. All I could do to roll over. Déjà vu and a concussion pounded like a jackhammer on my skull. Same black clothes, same strangefamiliar face, only missing the sneer. Cold comfort, since he held a thick baton above me.

Like moving through mud, I lifted my left hand defensively, tried to fumble for my gun with my right. He climbed atop me, his legs pinning my right arm against my side. I tried to shield my face, dodged the worst of it, heard more than felt the snap in my hand as fingers bent unnaturally.

I screamed, pulled my right hand free. Without the gun. All I could manage was to put it up between him and me, like a fighter trying to get off the ropes. He aimed a blow at my stomach. I twisted, caught it in the side, a small price to pay for dislodging him.

For all the good it did. I scrambled to my knees and he was already up, looming, baton ready to cause more damage if I reached for my gun.

The world was steadying a little. Not fast enough. Couldn't see a way out, so I put my hands up. I don't know if desperation or curiosity drove me.

"Why?" I asked. A simpler question than the ones I'd been digging into, or so I thought. I pressed my toes into the soles of my boots.

He paused, his weapon raised above his head. Blank-faced, like the answer was on the tip of his tongue. A long moment, indecisive.

"Traitor," he managed, swung. Telegraphed, or that would have been the big goodbye. I lunged. His blow glanced off my shoulder. I drove into his midsection, slammed him into the wall. Old brick. One impact or the other stole his breath. He bent double, managing to hold on to his club. Impressive, but too late. I swept his feet, dropped, wrapped my arm around his throat. He swung, wild, without strength. I held on until he was out. About that time the pain caught up, light-ning-bolts searing up from my broken fingers, nerve endings screaming.

I struggled not to pass out, scrambled to my makeshift dresser, pulled out the cuffs, and some-how had him in my chair, hands bound behind him, before he came to.

I was doing the best I could to splint my fin-gers when I heard him groaning. I ignored him for the moment. He must have chanced coming down the fire escape, so either brave or foolish. Hadn't kicked over the plants or fucked with my water collection. Lucky for us both. I let him take stock as I finished binding my fingers. The breaks looked clean enough. Hurt like August asphalt, but could have been worse.

The storm had refilled the collector. I drank long, felt a bit steadier. I could feel him watching me, so I let him see me pull the water from the source, then press it to his lips. He drank, offered a muttered thanks. I only nodded and sat on my mattress opposite, which made me small next to him, but I didn't trust myself to stand for long. The gun beside me would have to do.

"You probably already know I killed another one of you yesterday." His eyes widened. He didn't know, but he didn't look shocked, either. "Good. So you know I'm serious. We'll start easy. Who are you working for?"

That strange blank look again. "The trainer," he said. "I don't know his real name. But he helps us integrate." That meant nothing to me.

"Us?" I thought I knew.

"The others like me. Like Red. The one you killed."

Every word made my headache worse. "How many of you are there?"

"In my creche, there were four of us. We lost Yellow a while ago." He grimaced. "Now just two."

"Are there other creches?"

He shrugged. "I don't know. Never saw anyone but us and the trainer. He'd get messages sometimes. From his employer, I think."

I knew a thing or two about tells, a byproduct of navigating my father's anger. My captive seemed honest. Forthcoming, even.

"Who does he work for?"

"I have no idea." His eyes were on my gun. I wasn't going to shoot him in cold blood but hoped he didn't know that.

"You said I was a traitor. Why?"

This time his grimace was worse. Like it physically pained him. "I just know it. When I think of you . . ." He shut his eyes tight, breath ragged. "Treachery."

None of this made any sense. Nobody who's lived on the street since they were fifteen gets away clean. I'd done harm. Intentionally, accidentally, with good motives and bad. But who had I betrayed? The commune, some would say. And if the commune, then Kay, too. But they could barely keep their tech running. No way they were—what? Growing clones?

Between fears that clones would replace workers in what jobs remained and sanctity-of-life arguments from people both well-meaning and not, cloning was widely loathed. Growing conscious clones was illegal. The KC government made it a capital crime, and the militias, well, they'd make sure your death was slow in coming. Offshore, rich folks could buy replacement organs, and there were rumors of full mind transfers. Probably just rumors. Memory tech was one thing, but keeping one's selfhood intact? A nightmare. There'd been famous rogue attempts, with the subjects losing the thread of identity. Couldn't conceptualize themselves as their past—now dead—selves, couldn't escape that shadow.

But no one needed to solve that problem, not to make use of clones. This one didn't think he was me, didn't need to. Not hard to imagine the value of a blank-slate body, if you didn't mind the risk. Grab their organs, get some cheap labor for jobs not even the most desperate would take. Capitalists could always find use for new sources of flesh.

"Treachery," I repeated my clone's words. "Fine. Think about that. Maybe you'll remember something useful." Only one thread made sense. "Start with this. Your trainer, he works for Bio-Gesis, right?"

My clone's eyebrows raised. "I don't know." My finger twitched on the revolver's handle. He pulled back, nearly knocking his chair over. I lifted my hand away from the gun, raised my own eyebrow, inviting. Insisting.

"I've seen that word on supplies and equipment," he said. "But I don't know what it means."

Still sincere, almost painfully so, if I was any judge.

I dug further, but he knew next to nothing. I doubt "Red" had, either. He had a burner phone to check in when he was done, an app running on it that anonymized the device ID of his trainer. I considered sending a message, then tried to find something else I could use. When I finally gave up, he'd worked up the nerve to ask.

"Are you going to kill me?"

Killing him would be safest. But I had rules: the memories from my implant were for me and me alone. Help people when I could. Don't kill anyone who wasn't an active threat. "Not unless you give me a reason, kid," I said, though it was impossible to judge his age.

"They call me Blue," he said.

"Blue?" I followed an instinct. "Do you like that name?"

He blinked, shook his head, not quite a no. Like he wanted to chase away a fly.

"Think on that, too." I turned his chair so it was facing the corner. Only a few feet from me even there, but unless he was more flexible than I was, he'd not be able to watch me. Should be safe enough. I bolted the door, stacked the windowsill with some old-style real-glass cups I'd scavenged.

Fought sleep for a few hours, since I was sure as fuck concussed. Even considered dumping my augment's memory up to the cloud, but that was half a year's rent. No way to swing it.

Finally I did sleep, I think. In snatches. Even enhanced, I couldn't tell where wakefulness began or ended. The memory augment recorded and played back, nothing more. Only as good as the data I was feeding it. Sleep deprivation and a head wound were a bad combo. I added my memory to the long list of things I couldn't trust.

"Where are we going?" Blue asked. I'd cuffed his hands in front of him, draped him in a sheet to make that less obvious. I was a step behind, gun in my pocket, hand on my gun. A pill had eased the pain, but now my fingers itched under their bindings.

I'd taken us on a roundabout path, hoping to avoid any more killers lying in wait. Past the rotting husk of the arena where my father had once forced me to attend a political rally. A would-be president, talk of strength, sanctity, stability. Local cops and fascists running security. This man fighting with others for the job, and for what? To be the one in the nice office when the bill comes due?

"What do you remember?" I responded. "From before the trainer. The creche."

I imagined the tightening of his features, like he'd had the first flash of a migraine.

"I don't think . . . not memory. Just . . . knowing."

Something felt wrong, prickled the back of my mind. Like I was forgetting something. For years, a rare feeling. Didn't know what it meant. Nothing good. I wondered if this job would shake me to pieces. Not for the last time.

I wanted to ask if he knew what he was. He didn't talk like a child, but that didn't mean he understood he'd been crafted out of me. But questions like that might break him. Which might make things less complicated. Instead, I belatedly answered his question.

"We're not going anywhere you know." A chill, despite the heat. If he did? "A commune," I said. "You know what that is?"

"A group of people. Same root as community, communion—"

"Yeah, okay." Dead Gods, he unsettled me. "Things might work out for you if you behave." And if the commune agreed. Didn't love my odds. My plan wasn't great, but I couldn't think of anything better.

"My head hurts. I should have killed you." Blue gave neither sentence more emphasis than the other. "But I'll behave."

This was a terrible idea. But I didn't have a better one, unless dumping his body down a storm drain counted. Wouldn't do that, not unless he was an active threat. Every moment I spent back at the commune rubbed salt in old wounds, and this was far worse than me sharing a meal, crashing for a night. I figured they could just fucking deal with my presence for Kay's sake. But this was different. The favor I was about to request was huge. They'd be furious, and I couldn't blame them.

They'd call me a cop. Couldn't blame them for that, either.

There were two guards at the door. I didn't know the adolescent. Tattoos in the Diné language curved up their left arm, and the message on their knuckles read "Fuck Cops." Their shoulders were pulled wire-taut and a grim smile on their lips. We had something in common, then. Fury had been my constant companion as a teenager. Kept me alive. Hadn't stopped until the commune. Until Kay.

The other guard was Turner, his white hair in dreads, who'd looked sixty since I'd known him and was at least two decades older than that. Our oldest elder. A Black anarchist who'd survived, thrived, through terrible times. Maybe our most respected member. He could have had more influence, if he'd wanted it. I suspect he was trying to cultivate something in the community, something that would outlast him.

The younger guard turned to him. Turner looked between us. His eyes narrowed. Wary.

"I've got a guest I hope you can take in. Briefly," I said. Turner glanced at Blue's concealed hands.

"Em, better spread the word. We'll be wanting a meeting."

I could have simply gone in, made them stop me. But even I would push things just so far.

"I don't mean anyone harm, Turner," I said as we waited for Em.

"Hmmm," he said, and went quiet long enough I thought that was all. "Intentions only mean so much, Dora."

"I know." Couldn't argue with that. "And I'm sorry."

He nodded, kind enough not to remind me how little that was worth. After a while, Em came back out with Samuel.

"What's this about?" my old friend asked.

"Blue here needs a place to stay. I'll explain to the group."

"And if we decide against you?" From someone else, that would have been an insult. From Samuel it only hurt.

"I'll honor that, of course," I said, glanced at Blue. "Blue can speak for . . ." I'd been thinking of Blue as *him*, but couldn't say it. "For Blue."

"Come in, then," Samuel said, reluctantly. "Turner, I'd like to take over for you, if that's okay. They could use your perspective."

Closest thing I'd have to a sure supporter and he was staying outside.

The commune rearranged tables and gathered in a semicircle. Called up bad memories of lost arguments and a lost home. Of that last night, when I'd lost the argument and fucked off. It had felt so urgent, so justified, to leave it all behind. To be right and brave. We're at our cruelest when we're convinced we're righteous.

The room was too quiet, none of the usual laughter, bickering, quiet chatter. Their eyes on me, on Blue, then settling on Juan. So I knew who they'd picked to moderate.

"Dora, you've brought a *captive* to us?" Juan asked. A ripple of anger flowed through the room.

I grimaced. Most of the people in this room had done at least a little time, locked up for vagrancy, petty theft, dealing, protests. City jails or corporate-branded work farms: same shit, different uniforms. Not one of us approved of captivity. Hell, I'd bought the cuffs on Blue's wrists for sex.

As if the commune didn't hate me enough, now they thought I was a prison guard. I hated bringing my would-be murderer here. Didn't see any choice. Because the cops were our enemies. Because I had to either find a place for Blue or kill him. Because someone had severely fucked him up, and I knew what that was like. Because I needed to prove to myself that I wasn't as far gone as I feared.

"I hope I've brought you a guest. This is Blue." I pulled the sheet back, uncuffed him. Blue rubbed his wrists, his eyes darting. Took a seat.

"Someone sent Blue to kill me," I said. A tremor of noise from those gathered. "First they sent one of Blue's . . ." Brothers? Siblings? Fellow copies? "Coworkers. When that failed, Blue attacked me at home."

Plenty of anger, still, but I could see connections being made. Good. I didn't have a backup plan.

"Blue wasn't entirely in control of what happened. Even so, Blue could have killed me and didn't."

"So what's the problem?" someone demanded. A murmur of assent. Juan raised a hand, asking for silence. Got it.

"So why bring Blue to us?" Juan asked.

I turned to Blue. "If you have the chance, will you try to kill me again?"

I knew a mind at war with itself. I've been there. Seen that look in my mirror when I was twelve. My queer-ass self at war with the obsessive binaries of my father, the voice in my head telling me I was evil, deluded, a monster. Awful stuff I'm glad I don't remember clearly. Hated seeing something like that play out in this nightmare version of my face.

"I . . . I'm not . . . maybe?" Blue managed. Hardly an assurance that I was safe in his hands.

"I can't leave him at my place. Won't turn him

in. He's unarmed. He needs—we need—someplace to stay until I have answers."

"We don't keep prisoners!" someone shouted, and a murmur of agreement followed. Some fixated on what I'd done, others thinking maybe I had a point. They weren't keeping poker faces. I had to give them a reason to say yes.

"I'm not asking you to lock Blue up. Just . . . keep an eye."

"And if Blue decides to just walk out the door?" Turner asked. All eyes on him, then on me.

"Then I hope you'd warn me," I said. What else could I ask? Shoot him? Lock him away? These were free people.

Juan turned his attention to my clone. "Do you mean any harm to us, to anyone but Dora?"

"No!" Blue said firmly. "I'll follow your rules if you let me stay. I think that would . . . help." Dead Gods, what had BioGesis done to him? He was broken on some fundamental level. Couldn't be trusted to be in control of himself. But I was confident he wasn't lying.

Murmurs broke into clusters of conversation. My old community, doing the work. Debate, disagreement, seeking consensus. Or even understanding.

Juan stepped forward. "I think we'll want to

speak with Blue alone. You'd better wait outside."

I nodded. "Don't push too hard. Blue's . . . fragile."

"I'll do my best."

I scanned the room. Lylah was gesturing wildly, Samara listening with a frown. Valk looked terrified, and Juan exhausted. He was too levelheaded to punish me for my cruelty, but I doubted I could push him much further.

Outside, I pressed my body to the alcove wall, sheltering in the shade beside Em and Samuel.

"Tell me you have a secret twin." Samuel tried for a smile.

"It would have to be quintuplets."

I watched him consider the implications. "Fuck," he said. "Do you think this has anything to do with Kay?"

"A big coincidence, otherwise."

"Then what's the connection?"

"I don't know," I admitted. "I figure someone's going after the commune, but why like this?"

Samuel's eyes moved across my face. "How bad is it, Dora?"

Something in me broke a little. "Blue's . . . sibling, I guess. Jumped me in an alley. Had to kill him."

"Oh, Dora," he said, and held his arms for a

hug. I accepted. I'd had lovers since I left, but the arms of a friend? It had been longer than I'd like to admit.

Don't know what I'd have done if my phone hadn't buzzed. I muttered a thanks, disentangled. It was Styles, on CryptChat: "Found answers. Tonight, in person?" followed quickly by another text with a confirmation code. They'd learned well.

I confirmed, sagged back. "With luck, I'll know more in a few hours."

Samuel looked relieved, settled beside me. "I hope so." For the commune's sake, for Kay's, for mine? I didn't ask.

Juan came out almost an hour later. I stood up, tried to read his face.

"Blue can stay," he said. "For now." I guess I looked relieved. "Look, Dora, you being here. It's straining things." A massive understatement.

"I know. I'll get clear as soon as we have answers, Juan."

He hesitated, dropped his eyes. "We've taken in broken folks before. We'll do it again. I think Blue will be okay. But there's more than a few here who feel you're abusing the community agreements." The very agreements that I'd split with the commune over, feeling they didn't take safety seriously. That they put too much trust in strangers, in people who might mean us harm. Fix's dead body had said I was right, and I'd thought that was enough. But others felt my solution would have turned the commune into something worse, something that violated our most fundamental values. I lost the argument, called them fools, stormed out, and vowed never to return. So each time I relied on the agreements, it must have felt like a thumb in the eye.

I stared at him. "We've got a murderer loose. I was attacked at home, Juan."

He sighed. "I know, Dora, and I know you're trying to help." Hardly comforting. "But this, what you're doing—don't tear this family apart trying to save it."

The second time he'd made such a warning. This time I managed to keep my fool mouth shut.

I'd never set foot in the community lab. I knew Styles used it, and I'd helped with their security design without ever knowing its location. Safer that way. It was tucked in beside the back of a grocery store, in a neighborhood where technicians, nurses, and other folks with in-demand jobs lived. There wasn't much middle-class left, but from what I'd seen, where it remained was in places like this, with a little money, good corporate jobs, and an almost fanatical obsession with Nice Neighborhoods. The apartments had carefully presented facings: potted plants, some even real, on the windows; impeccably clean stoops; shiny, heat-reflective surfaces. All of it sent the message "We're nothing like those poor folks." Was it whiter than adjoining neighborhoods? Of course. At least the busy neighborhood made comings and goings easy to conceal. Styles met me at the corner, escorted me inside. The lab was one large room, all gray concrete and red brick, nearly half its space filled with server racks. No idea how they were getting that much power. Didn't ask. Need-to-know is the byword, always.

Just us and one other tech as Styles led me to a terminal, pulled up the results. A chart far too complex for me to read. They struck a series of commands and split the chart in two, each showing spikes and valleys. My father had worked with chemists when I was little, and back then he'd still held out hope that I'd be his brilliant heir, carry on his legacy. I could just about imagine that version of me: very masc, short-cropped hair, those old-school neckties he loved so much, staring at a computer on weekdays and going to church on the weekends. Just one more way I was a disappointment. But I knew a little about mass spectrometry.

"Okay," Styles said, pointing. "These peaks and valleys here, they're from the drug that was most of our sample. A prescription sedative, without any embedded lab markers. That means it was made on the street." No surprise there. Those were the only drugs most folks could afford. And a dead end.

"And this one?" I pointed to the split-off chart.

"There wasn't a lot of it left in the sample," they said. "I wasn't sure what I was seeing. Called in a favor to be sure." They brought up another screen. Clearly a photo from a powerful micro-scope. A series of digits etched on the side of a spiral shape. "This is corporate encoding. What we've got here is a designer drug, the real deal, not reverse-engineered."

That feeling of everything fitting together. "Let me guess. BioGesis?"

Styles glanced at me curiously. "No, actually. EvoTech."

I knew them, saw their corp label every day, even took one of their meds, but couldn't see how they fit in to Kay's murder. "EvoTech? Why would one of the big corps' drugs be in Kay's—?" I filed that question away. "Any idea what the drug is?"

Styles' grin said *of course I know*. "Hey, it's me. The branded name is Xynygen. It's used to treat—"

"—ARS." Fuck.

"Yeah. A devious choice. It's easy to OD on if you don't have the syndrome."

A feeling like someone sewed rocks into my intestines. I knew who'd killed Kay. I'd sat across from Kay's murderer and thought she was a victim. She'd even told me to my face that she had access to Xynygen.

"I owe you big, Styles," I said. "I've got to—to run."

And run I did.

If anyone at the commune had a personal device, I didn't know their numbers. Mostly they used burners when they had to. Affordable and safer. Usually. Now it meant I couldn't warn anyone about the killer among them. No wonder she'd seemed so crushed. Even had me chasing my tail, like a fool.

It was late night by the time I made it. I pushed past two confused guards. Quiet inside. A small cluster of people playing a card game looked up. I ignored them. In the community garden, two figures worked under a grow light, bent low. Juan and Blue. Both stared as I stormed past, up the stairs. Didn't take me long to find the right room. Like most, she'd chalked her name on the door.

"Valk!" I pounded on the door. No answer. Again, hammering, demanding. I felt sure I was too late, that she'd killed again, that she'd run. No response. Under the door, a light clicked off. Footsteps behind me, coming up the stairs. I drew my revolver, tried the door. It opened easy.

Pitch black in the room. The window, a square of less-dark. I stood exposed in the doorway, backlit by the LED lights of the hall. An easy target.

Movement inside, a figure pushing out the window.

"Stop!" I demanded. Raised my gun. They paused for a moment, outlined just enough to give me a shot. I didn't pull. Rushed at them instead— tripped over something, my gun skidding away. Something wet on my hands. I struggled to my knees, but they were gone.

The light clicked on. In the doorway, Juan and Blue, horror on their faces. I'd tripped over Valk. Two small, sharply-defined holes in her chest, another in her forehead. Blood everywhere. All over me.

I stumbled to the window. Someone had pulled off the boards, left their escape rope dangling. I was too late. The killer was gone.

When I turned around, Juan had my gun, and a crowd gathered in the hallway behind him.

"I know how this looks," I said, and vomited.

This time it may as well have been a trial. Which was good luck. Someone more impulsive than

Juan, or just someone who didn't want me to be innocent, might have shot me right there.

Further luck: my revolver hadn't discharged, no casings on the floor. The wounds Valk had taken went all the way through, left one needled round in her wall, and two more had gone clean through to the next room. An expensive and nearly silent mag-accelerated weapon had done this. And witnesses could confirm I'd just come in.

No one there had the fancy tech that would let them project my augment-stored memories, not that I'd have agreed to that, not even to save my neck. I'd loved this place, these people, but that didn't mean they had a right to my memories. So much had been taken from me, but those memories weren't for anyone but me.

None of them trusted me, but it was clear enough that I hadn't killed Valk. Harder was explaining what I knew about the case. Hardest was the desperation and fury on their faces.

I talked them through it as best I could. Valk had every reason to think that no one would look for an ARS drug in Kay's system. She'd had access to the drug through her mom. Should've been the perfect murder. Valk couldn't have known Kay would have an allergic reaction. Nothing big, just inflamed skin at the injection site. A bump I'd felt while holding her corpse.

The rest was harder. Why had Valk killed Kay? Who'd killed Valk and why? I had some ideas about the first part. Not so much about the second. "That drug's expensive," I told them. "And Valk's mom . . . well. My best guess is that Evo-Tech was holding it over her."

"She wouldn't have—" Samuel insisted.

"Anyone can be pressured with a weak point. Especially with loved ones' lives on the line," I said. "And who knows what they were telling her?"

"Let's say you're right, and EvoTech or whoever was behind this. Why target Kay?" Juan asked.

"I don't know." An angry ripple. Not my fault we were here, but I understood. I'd left because I was furious at what I saw as the community refusing to take its own safety seriously. I felt they'd chosen risk over protection. They believed I wanted order at the cost of freedom. Either I was a walking rebuke or proof that my way didn't work. Take your pick.

All I could do was push on. "But you can bet EvoTech is behind it. And they want something from this neighborhood."

"Even the dealers don't bother here," someone objected.

"Because someone's been paying them to leave. Or else." I told them about what I'd learned. More info than I wanted to share, but desperation left me without options. "We need witnesses. See what's going on. If we know what they're doing here, maybe we can stop them."

"So you say," Lylah said, then turned to the others. "We're just supposed to believe Valk was a killer? Why should we believe this woman? It's all thin connections and her own assertions. She could be involved. Or covering for someone."

Fury like a jagged blade tore through me.

"Who came in while you were on watch a couple nights ago, Lylah?" I demanded. The room went silent. "Someone here was meeting with a moneyed stooge. Couldn't see their face, but they must have gone right past you." I let that hang. She opened her mouth, and I pushed. "Unless you were the one at the meeting."

Lylah's lip curled. "I'm not a fucking snitch." She hadn't denied letting someone pass. Now all those eyes were on her.

Samara's quiet voice cut through the silence. "Valk's dead. You were right not to snitch, but now we need to know."

Clearing herself meant Lylah would have to back me. Couldn't fault her rage.

"Yeah, Valk came in late that night, drenched. What of it? We're free people. Most of us, anyway," Lylah said. But I was too tired to wound.

After that, there was a lot of talk, plenty of shouting, but no one thirsty for my blood. I got what I needed: the phone they'd found in Valk's pocket. Nobody seemed pleased, but better I snooped than they did. They sent me outside while they debated. I figured they'd argue for a while, then decide what to do with Valk's body. Not a thought I cared to linger on.

It wasn't hard to crack her phone. Mine had several custom apps for when I needed access to something I wasn't supposed to have. Had everything unlocked in under a minute. Probably hadn't occurred to her that anyone would try. She'd stored a number for "Him," no other name or title, and the most recent had been to confirm a meet for "The Usual Place, 1500." As simple a code as could be, just an inversion using the old twelve-hour clock. 1500 for 0300.

I scrolled back through. Nothing else to tell me what she'd been up to, though there were two other texts to arrange meets, both in the last couple months. Only "1500" had been marked urgent, so I took a shot, matching her texts' diction as best I could: "Request a meet." Marked it urgent, hit send. Slept a little, curled up there, ignored by and ignoring the guard. Got a response within the hour: "Usual Place, 1000."

2200, then. I confirmed, was thinking how I'd play it, when Juan emerged, Blue with him.

"We're finished," Juan said. The sky was bruising in the east, and I still had blood under my nails.

"Then can I get some sleep?"

Juan glanced away and I saw it all on Blue's face.

"Oh." When I'd left the commune, it had been spectacular and ugly. I'd committed emotional arson, then fled the scene. But it had been my call, and it left me unprepared for this.

"I'm sorry," Juan said. "It's not . . . it's not necessarily permanent. But the vote was clear." Which wasn't binding, exactly. *Bind* implies a hierarchy: binder and bound. But community agreements mattered. If they'd agreed they didn't want me there, I couldn't do shit about it without violating our core principles. No matter what they thought of me, that was a line I'd never cross. Even I, prodigal daughter or not, had left rather than defy the community. So there was nothing I could do.

I was fucked.

And I'd thought I was too exhausted to be hurt. I stared at my hands, palms up before me, like I was holding the key to all this. No such luck. Just two bandaged fingers sticking unnaturally straight, their wrappings stained with Valk's blood.

"Some of us voted to let you stay," Blue said.

I stared at him as my brain slowly processed that. He'd not been barred. Juan started to speak, thought better of it.

"Sure," I said. Lying isn't one of my vices, but I went on. "No hard feelings. Look, Juan, whoever's behind this, they aren't done with the commune. Don't let people think they're safe."

His look was sad enough to melt me.

I turned, headed out. Nothing else for it. Even if they hated me, my time at the commune had reminded me how much I'd loved it. Still did, in my way. And now it was gone. Again.

Only a block away, I heard feet rushing up. I turned, reaching to my side. It was Blue, unarmed, putting his hands up.

"Shit! Sorry," he said. "Didn't mean to . . . you know."

"What is it, Blue?" I asked. I figured if he was going to kill me, he'd just go for it, not try to put me at ease. As if that was even possible.

"I'd like to help you. If you want, I mean."

That surprised me enough to cut through my bone-weariness, my self-loathing. "What?"

"You're not giving up. On the . . . the murders, I mean. On whatever's happening to the commune?"

It hadn't occurred to me. I shook my head. "Not giving up."

"I didn't think so," Blue said. "Look, they'll send others. My brother. Soon, I bet. And whoever killed Valk is out there. You could use backup."

"You tried to kill me two days ago," I objected. "Aren't you still planning to kill me?"

"No. I mean, I don't think so. Part of me still wants to, uh, Dora, but not now, not while you're trying to . . . to stop this." Whatever his damage, he was sincere. Small comfort if whatever they'd done to him could snap him back to violence. If he didn't know his own mind.

Same could be said for all of us.

"Okay," I said. "Yeah, thanks." I did need back-up, even if it was from this nightmare version of me, this one who'd tried to end me. Even if Blue wasn't really himself. I'd have to trust him. A little. "I'll be back tonight, about 2000. We'll meet here. I've got a job for you."

He smiled. I'd never liked my smile, but his was open, pleased. Well. If he was going to kill me, at least he'd enjoy it.

I climbed to the roof of the building opposite mine, edged through the rooftop garden and past the water tanks. Watched my window for a long time. No movement. Approached my door, quiet as I could, listened long, pressed my belly to the floor, peered beneath the door. No movement, no sound. At some point there's no choice. I readied my .38, then turned the key and pushed the door open in a single motion. It slammed into the wall on my right. No one hiding there. No one pressed against the wall on my left, either. The studio quiet, no more torn-up than I'd left it. I edged over to the bathroom. The door partly open. I crouched, rammed my knee into it.

Old plywood crunched, and the door hammered against the wall. No one inside. I locked the front door, stacked some pots in front of it for noise. Checked the window again. No movement outside. Alone.

I poured water, sniffed it, imagining poison. It smelled of mildew, as ever. Nothing else. Couldn't survive without water, so I chanced it. Even warm, it felt great. I'd pushed hard and could feel the reckoning coming for me like a loan shark. I hoped I could put down a payment, hold off the balance coming due for a while longer. Devoured a couple tins of NutriPaste, almost too hungry to notice the sweet-over-bitter taste, grabbed my pillow, locked myself in the bathroom, bracing the door from the inside with my chair. That didn't leave much room, but I'd slept in worse places. I knew that every noise from another apartment, every dead face that pushed its way up through my memory, would put my body on alert.

Even so, sleep came on like a snap.

Turns out that being closeted is bad for you. Shocking, I know. My early adolescence is mostly dissociation, my memory not so much full of holes as it was an ocean on which a few vivid remembrances float. The face of my mother crying over some horror of the world she'd tried to shield me from. Birdsong in the mornings—there'd been birdsong, then, truly. Drinking my fill of water, clear and cold. The road thick with cars, gas and electric. Fleeing some disaster or traveling to some marvelous place. My father drilling me on some obscure scientific concepts, as if through cleverness or force of will he'd craft me into a scholar, shape me into a worthy heir. It was doomed to fail, and through the maelstrom of my memory his severe face rose, stubborn and intractable and fighting the realization that I'd never be what he wanted. He'd always been quietly furious. At himself. At my mother. At me, a disappointment even before I stopped pretending to be his son.

Even when I finally got clear, no end to the fragments of suffering; my father's emotional vise grip traded for bad nights on the street, horrors suffered and violence inflicted. Learning how to defend myself. I learned it well. At great cost. Hunted by predators, harassed and worse by cops, locked away for solicitation, which is to say for being visibly trans.

I did lots of unpleasant things to earn cash for my augments, but it was better than the fog I'd had before. Not as good as estrogen, though.

I got picked up once after the memory implants. Only time I had a lawyer, a blond guy with an expensive suit, a Texas accent. He wanted to enter my implant's stored memories into evidence, since the cops' augments had experienced "interference." A test case, he said. Poor guy really believed the system could be fixed. Offered his services pro bono if I gave them access to my memories, my traumas. Shit, no.

So I did the time, kept my memories private. There's stuff in my head that only I will ever know. The point isn't what I suffered.

It's that some of us survive. Somehow, even now.

Way back in the mind-fog, long before the implants, someone told me dreams were part of the process of building long-term memories. Explains why a side effect of memory augments is vivid dreams. The past came clawing, its talons scratching on the insides of my eyelids.

I woke up screaming. Flailed and jammed my

broken fingers against the sink. Screamed some more.

My neighbor banged furiously on the wall. In the commune, people would have come running to ensure I was safe. The pain of their absence almost as sharp as the one shooting up my arm.

Blue was waiting for me at the corner.

"You're sure about this?" I asked.

"Yes," he said.

"And you're not going to kill me?"

"Not today," he said, serious as a mastiff guarding her pups.

I handed him Red's gun.

"Safety's here," I said. "Did they give you any training?"

He shrugged. "Some."

I didn't trust a damned thing they'd told him.

"Don't point it at anything that you're not prepared to kill. Keep the safety on until you need it. And don't shoot yourself."

Ideally, I'd take him down by the river, teach

him to shoot. No time for that.

"Got it," he said.

I filled him in on what I needed from him: very little. "Thanks, Blue."

He tilted his head like a puzzled dog. "You're welcome. And, uh, Dora, I know that I'm your clone or whatever. In case you were worried." I had been. Squeeze an egg top-to-bottom and it can take it, but tap a crack into the side . . .

"Uh, good to know," I said. "You should know it's illegal. Cloning conscious people, I mean. That's not on you, but it could blow back."

He was silent, considering. "I think . . . I think I need to be careful about trust."

"Wise." I wondered which of us was more foolish to trust the other. "You ready?"

He was.

I leaned against a brick wall, hood pulled low. Full dark, but even so there wasn't much chance Valk's contact would mistake me for her. That wasn't the point. I was pretty sure I knew who

Valk had been working for. They'd show up because they'd want answers. Same as me.

Sure enough, two gleaming eyes in the dark marked Smith's arrival. He picked a spot a few feet from me, hands in pockets.

"Valk's dead," I said.

If I'm any judge, he was disappointed, but not surprised.

"Did you kill her?" he asked.

"No," I said. "Did your people?"

"No," he said. "Nothing in it for us. We limited her exposure. She shouldn't have been a target."

"So who did?"

His bright eyes narrowed. "I didn't know she was dead until you told me."

"But you know what's going on," I said. "You were the one extorting her."

Smith scoffed. "Extortion? It was a business arrangement."

"'Work for me or your mother dies' is hardly free association."

He shrugged, not bothering with a denial. "She told you?"

"She didn't have to. EvoTech drugs killed Kay."

He hid his surprise quickly, but not quick enough.

"Did you order Valk to kill her?"

"Absolutely not." He seemed sincere. But it wasn't like he would cop to the crime.

"I don't believe you. Tell me what she was doing for you. And what this is all about."

"You know I can't do that," Smith said. A hint of motion behind him.

"Two people are dead because of your corporate games, Smith." I raised my voice. Not much, but I let my fury into the words. "Don't push me."

"You're smarter than this, Theodora. I'm an operative. You know I don't have the answers you need."

"You have some of them, I bet," Blue said, and pressed his gun to the back of Smith's head. Gratifying to see Smith stiffen.

I pulled my .38. "Hands up. Go slow." Smith obeyed at once, hands empty, palms out.

"Killing me would be bad for your health," Smith said.

"I'm caring less and less about that," I said, glanced past him to Blue. "What about you?"

"Less and less," he said.

I kept a close eye on Smith's hands as he did the mental math.

"We were compensating Valk for a service:

gathering intel on whatever BioGesis is doing here," the operative said. "That's all. Did she strike you as a killer, Theodora?"

Not even a little. But they don't always. I shook my head.

"Here's the truth," Smith went on. "My employer—and I'm not saying who they are—wouldn't have wanted Kay removed. By now you know that BioGesis is after full control of this neighborhood."

I didn't know that. It fit with the evidence, but EvoTech could have been playing me. Kept that to myself. "Go on."

"When we met last, Valk said she thought Kay had been compromised."

My fists clenched. "No fucking chance."

The hint of a smile on Smith's lips. "Come now, Theodora. Everyone has weak points. You of all people should know that." I did know it, had said something similar recently. Didn't make it easier to take.

"Are you trying to get shot?" I asked, struggling with calm. He glanced at his raised hands.

"Poor choice of words," Smith allowed. "Valk didn't say how she knew. She was about to snap under the pressure, so I didn't push."

Blue's eyes were wide, unsure. This wasn't as comfortable as attacking me had been. Unsettling, to see my own fears mirrored back at me. I did my best to project confidence.

"We're on the same side here, Theodora," Smith said after a long moment.

"We're really not."

"You persist in being difficult. Our goals are currently aligned, then. I want to know what BioGesis is doing, and you want answers, and an end to the violence. It doesn't matter if Kay was turned. Valk thought she was and killed her. Even if my employer wanted Valk dead, we'd have just arranged a meet, done it there."

I frowned. Something about Valk's actions still didn't quite add up. Even if she was convinced Kay had been turned, would she have committed cold-blooded murder? But Smith's version of events lined up pretty well. At the very least, I couldn't imagine Smith bothering with that elaborate B&E shit. That was more my clones' style.

Oh, *shit*.

Smith pressed his advantage. "Someone decided Valk was a problem and took her out. Either because she killed Kay—"

"—or because of something she knew." It did

make sense. Too much sense.

"Exactly. Look, Theodora, this is escalating. You can see that. And you've figured out that killing doesn't benefit my employer. Find out what BioGesis is doing, and I can provide material support if you need it. Plus compensation."

I hated this, but I needed to think. If it had been there, plain as the nose on my face, the whole time? Couldn't let Smith see my distress and put anything together himself.

"Okay," I said. "But if you're double-crossing me—"

"Please," Smith said. "Don't embarrass yourself. I know you'd kill me if I killed your ex." He dropped it in casually, just a reminder of his resources, his knowledge. "You know how to reach me."

Hands still up, he walked away, into the darkness.

Blue stared at me. "What's wrong, Dora?"

Vertigo. I stumbled, eased myself down curbside. Sat with my head in my hands. Think, Dora, think.

Blue's body beside me, a tentative clasp on my shoulder. When I didn't pull away, his arm draped around me. Holding me there. His gun sat on the pavement between us. I'd left it unloaded, of course.

Worked to pull myself together, to make sense of the blurred line between evidence and paranoia. Eventually gathered myself enough to speak.

"Are you still in?"

Blue nodded. "Yes, I am. It's like, you know, when your hands aren't free, and all you can think about is how much your nose itches? That's how this has got me."

"Me too."

My fingers itched unceasingly.

Blue insisted on staying with me. "If you die now, I never get to scratch the itch," he'd said. We walked under a patina of stars. When I was a kid, there'd been plenty of power to go around. Motherfuckers were still burning coal in those days, and wind power was online, solar. Don't know where the money was coming from, but KC at night lit up day-bright. Back then, you'd had to look close to see the rot of the long twentieth century. Now it lay exposed. But at least the stars had returned. "How much did they tell you about me?" I asked Blue. "Before they sent you out."

"Your name. Where you lived. A photo. That you were dangerous," Blue said.

"That's it?"

"Yes."

"Then why'd you call me a traitor?" I wished I'd asked when I could see his face, even though he seemed incapable of lying.

He was silent for so long I thought he was refusing—or unable—to answer. "You asked me about my memories. It's like that, a little. I don't remember a childhood. I didn't have an education. But I know things—like it's 'an' education, not 'a' education. Or language, etymology . . . I know you're a traitor in the same way I know those things." A long pause. "I mean, I *don't* know that. But I felt like I did."

My turn to pause. "Just felt like?" The night was quiet, a sliver of moon in place of rich folks' lights on the clouds.

"It's there still, Dora," Blue said. "Like an instinct. But not the only one, and I don't have to follow instincts."

My gut told me he'd been designed to do exactly

that. Couldn't say why. But no way he'd been designed to get in good with the commune, either. Surely not. That would require him failing to kill me, me taking him there, them accepting him. Too much chance. Blue—part of Blue—was off his leash.

"Well, thank you for not killing me. Yet."

Was that a flash of a smile in the dark? "Thank you for not killing me," he replied. "Yet."

No one waiting to jump us in the apartment. Just my solar fan pushing back a little of the heat. A little water for both of us and some cheap nutrient bars passed for dinner. Their grit stayed on my tongue for ages, and they tasted of salt and regret. Blue watched me, curious.

"You can ask me." I unlaced my boots, considering the relative merits of sleep and stims. Every attempt to gather my thoughts ended badly. Sharp thinking or unconsciousness each might help. Or make things worse.

"Ask you what?"

About being trans. About my body. The kinds of questions a certain type of person always came around to. "Whatever you want."

"Okay. Why are your eyes a different shade from mine?"

I blinked. My mouth gaped like a drowning fish. "What? No, same color." Muddy brown, I'd always thought.

"No," he said. "Here, look, I'll show you." In the bathroom, we stared at the mirror. The cut of the light and lack of sleep made grottos of my eyes.

"They're the same," I said. Mine more blood-shot, was all.

"No," Blue insisted. "Yours have these—these flecks. They're almost gold. Almost."

I stared into the mirror. Kay had liked the flecks in my eyes, too. Never really saw what she did. Still didn't. I stared at Blue, and they were there, not quite gold, but the promise of it.

"You have them too," I said. He shook his head hard. To my shock, his cheeks were wet. "What's wrong, Blue?"

"I don't know," he said. "Only—you're—you're—" I saw it in his eyes, no mistake. Delusional, sure, but there all the same. Though I'd rarely looked worse.

"I'm not," I said. But he was already leaning close. I let him. His beard scratched against my cheeks, not entirely unpleasant. He kissed too softly. I urged him on, my arms pulling him in. Yielding, caught in whatever he saw in me.

His hands on me, not as clumsy as you'd think, his lips ghosting over my throat. He didn't smell like me. Under our layers of sweat, his scent was like tilled earth. Heady.

Fingers on the hem of my tank top, lifting. My hands went above my head, tossed the top away, ignoring the jolt of pain from my fingers. He stared like a supplicant. "Gorgeous," he said. My heart was a bird battering itself against its cage.

He pulled me towards the mattress, but I stopped him, hands on his chest. His eyes wide, uncertain. "I can't," I said. "We can't."

"Oh." His gaze scanning my face, trying to understand. "Okay. Can I ask why?"

I'd forgive you for thinking it was because he was my clone. But there was a much bigger problem.

"You're a child," I said. "How old are you anyway?"

Blue grimaced. "I'm an adult. Old enough to carry a gun. To have your back. To make my own choices." He'd pulled back. I crossed my arms over my breasts, struggled to look at him.

"You want this?" I asked, at last.

"Yes," Blue insisted. "If you do."

I stood skewered. "I do," I said. "We'll stop anytime you say." He was kissing me again, and then we tumbled onto the mattress. He sprang ready as I peeled off his jeans, so eager. I slowed down, let the moment build. Moved over him, kissing, exploring, silently promising, testing where our favorite spots merged and diverged. Soft sounds in his throat rewarded me, his body like my childhood home mapped with alien cartography.

His hands knotted in my hair, oh-so-gentle, each cry from his lips urging me to guide, to control. When he'd been drawn tight as a bow, I put him on hands and knees, prepared him.

"I'm going to enter you now," I told him, adjusting myself, spreading lube. "If you want me to. Do you?" My nails charted a course down the curve of his back.

"Yes," Blue gasped. "More than anything. Please."

I went slowly, giving him time to adjust. To decline. He urged me on.

He wanted to be guided, controlled, and I was happy to provide. Later, when he'd recovered, I let him take me as I clutched him, his face alive with joy. His eyes gold-flecked, even if he couldn't see it.

Neither stims nor sleep, as it turned out.

We spent the next day hunting through the neighborhood, desperately searching for any sign of BioGesis's presence. Moving through the abandoned buildings, the old drug houses, townhouses whose residents had left without their children's toys, without their clothing. Just a more deserted version of the neighborhood I'd known, a place briefly warped by money, then by its sudden absence, and now by BioGesis. Had to be. But nothing pointed to the kind of operation I was now certain BioGesis was running. Far as I could tell, they'd only cleared people from a handful of blocks. That narrowed the search area. For all the good it did. If they were here, there must have been a footprint. Evidence.

At least the search kept my mind occupied. It helped me avoid thinking too much about what Blue and I had done. Didn't feel like incest to me, but sure as fuck not like masturbation, either. But the rest—what we were to each other, the foolishness of making that connection, the fear that

I'd taken advantage of him—clung to me like a shroud. The search was less fraught, even if it remained every bit as useless.

By late afternoon, dark clouds boiled up from the west, pushing cool wind ahead. A shelf cloud raced towards us like an open maw. This storm would put the last one to shame.

As Blue peered through a crack into one of the abandoned buildings, I investigated a long-abandoned storefront, pressing my cheek to the plywood, listening for voices or the rumble of machines, anything to point BioGesis's way. I didn't think there was anything special about this neighborhood, not to them. They were protecting an investment. But if they were making clones, there'd be signs. Had to be, I told myself.

The specter of Kay's face rose in my memory. OD'ing, dying without so much as someone to hold her. And the violation of what they'd done to her. What I suspected they'd done.

No need to turn anyone. Just replace them.

The more I thought about it, the more it was the only thing that made sense. But who had they gotten to, and how would I know?

Worse, every time I looked at Blue, I wondered if I'd been their first test subject, a proof-of-concept before they'd moved against the commune. It still didn't add up, but I felt the missing data like slivers under my skin, working their way deeper.

Fuck off with the self-pity, Dora.

They had to be operating out of the neighborhood. This wasn't something they'd do at that lovely campus of glass and steel. Not even the cops they'd bought could be sure to look the other way when it came to cloning, and if the militias found out—well. I took some comfort in knowing those fascists would kill Smith almost as eagerly as they'd kill me, though for different reasons.

Only problem was, I couldn't find a trace of them. Hard to imagine they'd be working out of vacant apartments like some second-rate crew. The bigger buildings, the ones that had been apartments and shops and then smaller apartments and then left to rot? Might be.

I looked for connections, checking old deeds from back when they might have meant something, even calling in a favor a cop owed me. Getting that favor had cost me dear. Felt terrible using it, like I always did when I had to work with cops. Even worse, it didn't help. The cops didn't even know there'd been months of systematic exit from the neighborhood. Why would they? They didn't even bother to roll by unless they were hunting a big bounty. They stayed mostly in the cluster of neighborhoods with money, guarding the gates from inside and out, presumably offering something to what remained of the middle class. They'd venture out occasionally, sure, mostly into blocks adjacent to wealth, making sure that people of color, poor folks, desperate outsiders, and those who were doing their best to hang on even as the world crumbled away—that none of us disturbed their patrons.

There was nothing to find. No one to turn to, unless EvoTech counted. Not so different from how I ended up being owed a cop's favor: sometimes all you can do is pick which devil to deal with.

"You're sure you don't remember anything?" I asked Blue. "Like, first sights from when they sent you after me? Nothing?"

Blue shook his head. "They blindfolded me, put me in a vehicle. I asked to be dropped off near your apartment. That's all I know."

I sighed. Four square blocks we'd searched, and nothing. There wasn't much more we could do, not without a real commitment to B&E, which I was seriously contemplating.

There weren't private cars in these neighborhoods, at least not any that hadn't been left to rust, and not many left in the city. Not with roads crumbling everywhere except a few arteries the city government managed to keep open, the ones that allowed deliveries to and from corporate enclaves, or to the highways where self-driving trucks raced along their routes. That meant whatever vehicle they'd used was likely some delivery truck, or it would have attracted too much notice. Which meant . . .

"They could be using one of these old warehouses," I told Blue, "but we'd see solar panels, or active power connections, or *something*." I had no idea what an operation like this required. But from Blue's account they had enough support for his creche, their trainer, some security. And I suspected that was the tip of the iceberg. But even assuming a small operation, they couldn't escape the need for power, for supplies.

You hid something like that in a busy place. Like the community lab by the grocers. Not in a mostly abandoned neighborhood. And yet they had to be worried about discovery. Why else go to all this trouble? I couldn't make sense of it. My thoughts went in circles, horrifically sluggish. My father had assumed my terrible memory also applied to my other cognitive skills. The implants had fixed the memory issue, and I'd always been able to count on my deductions. Until now. Until I desperately needed it.

Blame myself, feel shitty for making it about me, rinse, repeat.

Someone told me that old cliché came from how people used to shower. Might be true. When I was little, some people still had green lawns. Regular folks, not just the rich who wasted water to prove they could.

Blue brought me back to the present. "Rain's coming," he said, and sure enough the first spatters sizzled against the pavement.

"Gonna be a bad one." Lightning, cloud-to-cloud, overhead, punctuated my instinct. "We can call it for the night, if you want."

Blue tilted his head. "No, I'm good. I think doing this is—I think I need to." Easy to imagine him using this task to hold off whatever instinct they'd give him. Like he'd done last night, transmuting hatred into lust.

Like me, pretending this job could repair everything I'd broken.

My break with the commune started with horror, the kind not even my father's cruelties or those years on the street could brace me for. Usually, the violence came from the militias, or the cops, which at least made a certain kind of sense. This time it came from one of our own. A new member of the community, a scrawny ginger guy with a slow drawl, called himself Wilshire. He'd helped with the labor, seemed unremarkable, and whatever simmered beneath his surface, I'd missed it. We all had, until it was too late. Until Fix was dead, and Mills nearly so, and when we'd finally pulled Wilshire away from the carnage he'd caused, he sat blood-covered and sobbing.

Worst part? It was on my watch. The commune had asked me to do the job, and I'd missed this. Failed to account for what I knew, what I'd let myself forget. That every community has its predators, that letting in anyone, even if they had no one to vouch for them, was a sure way to get people killed.

Fix was dead. He'd been one of ours, my friend. To see him murdered by someone who'd broken bread with us, who we'd claimed as one of our own? Couldn't handle it. I've done plenty which haunts me in the dark, violence and emotional cruelty, words meant cruelly or kindly that left wounds. But Fix's death ate at me in new ways. Ripped something from my chest and left me bleeding. He'd been my friend. His safety had been my responsibility.

First thing you learn when you work in security is that no amount of preparation and caution can prevent violence, that cruelty and malice are diseases with reservoirs in the human heart that can never be eradicated. But I'd been the acting center of the security committee, the one tasked with keeping us safe, and I'd been unable to.

So I told the commune what had to change. In my expert opinion.

I'm not a complete fool. I knew my insistence grew out of loss, out of a sense of failure, but I'd already been convinced our commitment to voluntary association shouldn't require us to always open our doors to strangers, that we should enforce trial periods and community sponsors for those who wished to become permanent members.

Maybe I'd inherited some of my father's need for control. And even I knew that what I wanted ran dangerously close to coercion, to hierarchies of power. To a betrayal of what it meant to be an anarchist. But standing near a cliff isn't jumping over it, I told myself. And I'd long worried about our lack of safeguards, and the loss of Fix left me feeling that a) I had an obligation to try to change things, or b) I could exploit an opportunity. Choose one or both.

Ever since the nineteenth century, when some anarchists first threw bombs, people have assumed we hate order. (Funny how they never said that about the governments who launched much bigger bombs.) It's rulers we hate, not order. Any anarchist group spends more time than you might believe deciding what principles and mutual agreements they will operate by.

And to me, this principle was obvious: we didn't have a system that adequately reduced the risk of outsiders infiltrating and doing harm.

So I made my case to the community. It seemed so self-evidently wise that I was stunned when it was met with skepticism, and shaken beyond words when Kay spoke against it, never mind that we were partners. Never mind that I loved her like I'd never loved anyone before or since, and she knew it, and loved me, too. Hers wasn't the only voice or the loudest raised against me, but it was the one that clawed its way into my guts.

"We shouldn't do this, Dora," she said. "We *must* not do this. I don't know exactly where our line should be, but this crosses it. Requiring people to prove themselves to enter our community? Putting members in charge—*in charge*—of sponsoring them or turning them away? Making inner and outer communities? That's what militias do. What *states* do." Her eyes were red, her voice breaking, but she stared directly at me. And me, fucking dumbass with a memory implant? I remember every detail. "No matter how you dress it up, it's coercion, Dora."

"It isn't," I insisted, humiliated and angry. "Not if it's our consensus. Just one more choice about voluntary association. It's no different from any other community agreement."

Fool that I was, I still expected to win the argument.

"We're free people." Kay looked at me like I'd become unrecognizable. "Everyone here abides by the community agreements, and then they're welcome here for as long as they want to remain part of the community. If they break the trust of the community, we deliberate and maybe we ask them to leave." She shuddered, head to toe, sank to her knees. "We're all grieving, Dora. But what you're talking about? Writing systems of power into our agreements? Full members and partial ones? Hierarchies of membership? I'm begging you to reconsider."

She hadn't looked at anyone besides me, even though I'd asked for deliberation. I was the only one she was trying to convince.

Part of me wanted to do as she asked. A large part. But Fix's body rose like a specter from my memory, and I knew with dreadful certainty that I could never let what happened to Fix happen to Kay. Whatever risks to my safety I might expect, hers was too important. Too important for me to yield. Too important to compromise on.

"I will not withdraw it." My words were formal, my tone ugly. "I'm still the acting center of the security committee, and I urge this community to adopt my resolution and keep us safe."

Kay stared at her hands and said nothing else.

Not everyone was against me, but there was nothing close to consensus, and most were clearly going to side with Kay. Very soon it was obvious my resolution was doomed.

"You fools can stay and wait for disaster," I told them. "But I'll be damned if I'm going to be any part of it. I'm fucking done." Might say I scorched the earth.

Even so, as I packed my things, Kay begged me to stay, at least for the night. "Don't rush into this, Dora," she choked out through sobs. "Please. Sleep on it. In the morning we can talk about it . . ."

By then I only wanted her to hurt as much as I did. And my cruelties are sharp, professional.

"I won't stand by while you do this." I pulled my bag over my shoulder, seething. "I withdraw my consent."

I left her with her head buried in her hands. And went into exile.

The storm skipped twilight, and night slammed like a door. Blue and I moved furtively, two figures ducking between cover, as the tempest lit the sky and shook the ground.

Blue shivered beside me, blowing into his

hands, water dripping from his ears, his drenched beard.

"Hey, Dora?" he said. I had to lean in to hear. "I think . . . I think maybe I want to be called 'Theo' for now."

I guess I'd expected something like that, but not so quickly.

"Thanks for telling me, Theo."

I don't assume I know strangers' genders. But with Theo I had. Maybe I figured that if he was a man, that was a clear gulf between us. Making Theo's life about me. Objectifying. Even last night. Fuck.

"Do you have pronoun preferences?" I asked. "Like, which pronouns I should use to refer to you?"

Theo considered. "I don't—I'm not sure."

"Usually when I don't know someone's pronouns, I default to they/them until I learn. Would you like that? Or I can avoid pronouns entirely."

"Maybe just avoid them? It's all too much."

I clasped Theo's shoulder. "You're doing great, Theo. Better than you know."

Couldn't help but think that, mindfucked and all, I liked my clone's version of Theodore/a/ix better than mine.

Theo's smile wasn't locked up, restrained. On that face, joy looked like a reasonable expectation. I couldn't imagine what that felt like. Hadn't felt anything like it in the years since I left the commune. Didn't love that realization.

"You know, you're pretty great, Dora."

"You could've killed me, Theo, and you didn't." That was me, trying to take a compliment. Theo was still shivering, so I offered an arm, and we huddled together. A waterfall curtained us, spilling from the awning above. I remembered what it had been like, to finally be away from home. Both our homes were cruel places, but with familiar cruelty. Known. Now Theo faced the unknown, eyes sunken with lack of sleep, the storm concealing and revealing the clouds of our breath against the cold—

"Oh fuck," I said, so loud Theo jumped.

"What is it?" Theo looked around like someone expecting a hit squad. Not unreasonable.

"I know why we can't find BioGesis. I know where they are."

I didn't. Not exactly. But it had been there all along, if I'd thought to see it. A night soaked in cold rain. Steam rising from manholes, from storm drains. Something down there putting off lots of heat.

BioGesis's operation was underground.

Theo borrowed the tools we'd need from the commune while I waited at the corner, ignoring the eyes of two guards, their huddled forms revealed with each lightning strike, then cast again into afterimages that stayed with me whichever way my head turned.

BioGesis wasn't hard to find, once we were below. Reeking water flowed fast, nearly past our boots, small and not-so-small creatures skittered away from our lights. We found steaming pipes, followed them until they disappeared into a wall. From there it was just finding access. I pulled helplessly at the lever for an old metal door, which didn't budge until Theo pulled with me. Finally it groaned, then screeched on ancient hinges as it opened. If anyone was listening, they would know we were coming. I drew my gun. Theo followed my lead.

This hall was dry, a metal grating clanging underfoot, a light layer of dust showing no one had come this way recently. Around the corner, we found a metal door, a security camera above it, plenty of footprints from further down the passageway leading to and from it. This door was new, no rust, no adornment, just a glowing security pad.

"I don't suppose you know a passcode?" I asked.

"No," Theo said. "Sorry."

"Don't worry about it." I pulled out my phone, hunting for the pad's offer of a handshake. If this was high-end corporate tech, I'd be SOL. No way my apps could hack that. We'd report to Smith, hope that EvoTech's play settled the score. The wise option. I hated it.

I was lucky. Or unlucky. They hadn't bothered with elite tech here. I let my app work at the brute-force approach.

"They may know we're here," I said. They almost certainly did.

"What do we do?" Theo's hand ran through the beard, came away wet.

"I'll check it out," I said. "Stay here. If I'm not back in twenty minutes, get back to the commune, tell them what we found, then make contact with Smith."

Theo grimaced. "I'm not sending you in there alone."

Not for a moment did I consider letting Theo come with me. (*Let:* what a monstrous thought.) It was one thing for me to throw my last dice here, another to send Theo into that reckoning. No reason to get Theo killed too.

There's a joke in here somewhere about a trans woman afraid to change. Not very funny.

"You can't," I said. "If your creche is in here, you're a liability. Who knows what safeguards they have?" I didn't want to tell Theo what I feared, but I couldn't think of another way to keep my clone out of harm's way. "They could use you against me."

I knew that look, had seen it in the mirror. Fury with nowhere to put it. I'd used a dirty trick, no less so for its truth.

The anger passed over Theo's face, leaving a tight smile. "Be careful, Dora. No one else gets to kill you."

I gave a probably unconvincing smile. I didn't have the time or emotional reserves to figure out what we were to each other, but I liked Theo. Liked the naivety, kindness, the way Theo could still hope for something better. Should have said something, been honest with my clone. Couldn't manage it.

I unlocked Valk's phone, opened the messaging app, passed it to Theo. "Twenty minutes. Then tell the commune, contact Smith."

The security pad beeped. The door slid open. No security team waited for me with guns drawn, no smirking mastermind turned around in his chair. Just a simple hallway leading deeper. I was less than a block from the commune, old stone walls around me. They'd sealed off the surface access to old basements, connected them to the maintenance tunnels. No wonder we never saw them coming or going. Very secure. Somewhere, maybe a couple blocks away, they'd have an exit through an abandoned warehouse. Me, I'd have still preferred hiding an operation in a crowd. But this plan had worked for them.

Ahead of me, the hallway split into a T. No signs guided my way. I leaned out, checked both directions. More cameras on the ceiling, red-lit, but no sign anyone was coming for me. I went right. Came to another blank door, another glowing pad. Running a similar algorithm, apparently: my app cracked it in seconds.

You can expect to see something and still not be ready for it. Vats spread out before me, containing human shapes at all stages of development floating in milky liquid. Like something out of a horror vid, only flatly lit by old-fashioned LEDs, as though robbing it of visual interest could make it mundane. What shook me wasn't the clones, asleep, their bodies like figures in fog. I'd expected something like that, but hadn't been prepared for the number of vats. Four rows, each stretching at least a dozen units deep. Couldn't help myself. I looked. Some of the clones had my old face, others were no one I knew. In the second row, a nearly full-grown clone of Kay. A backup. I staggered, stomach twisting, and swallowed down vomit.

There are times you pray you're wrong, even knowing you aren't. By all the Dead Gods, they'd *replaced* her. Sent a clone in to undermine us— undermine the commune—from the inside. How long had her double lived among them? At the church I grew up attending, they'd have called it profane. For the first time in many years, I felt a truth in that word. They had violated something that should be absolute. Not by cloning, but by creating a version of Kay to undo all she'd believed in.

And Valk. Fuck, Valk, who knew Kay as well as anyone (except me, a selfish-as-shit voice in my head whispered). Valk, who was compromised by

Smith, desperate to save her mom. Who realized what had happened and taken it upon herself to fix it. What must it have been like, to kill a person wearing the face of your best friend? To go through the aftermath alone, unable to tell anyone what you knew, what you'd done, because if you did, everyone would know you'd been compromised? Horrific.

And someone, probably BioGesis, had killed her for it.

Rage and grief flooded me. I think if there'd been a power switch to flip, a way to end the existence of those clones in that moment, I'd have done it. There was none, not even a hammer with which to shatter housings until someone showed up to end me. My gun didn't have nearly enough shots. I forced myself onward. Still no one in the hallway. Either their security was abysmal, or I was walking into a trap. The smart money was on trap.

I was past caring. I meant to have this done, one way or another. The next room was an empty barracks, pristine bunks carefully made and waiting for their occupants. The next was the same, only with bare mattresses. No wonder they'd chased off the neighborhood. They were gearing up for a much bigger operation, and they didn't want an audience. Clever. Who would look for a clone op in the KC ghetto?

I needed to find the power source. I could end this all, or anyway, most of it. Unclench the knot in my chest, even if it killed me. No more dead friends, dead loved ones. A clean end. Just let me have my reckoning. I'd have prayed it if I believed anyone was listening.

A door at the end of the hall, seamless with the wall. Unlocked, like the dorms. I shouldered it open and the silence of the hall was replaced with a cacophony. Like a million people whispering at once, words I couldn't quite make out coming from every angle, from every dark corner. A circular room, and in the center a projected globe flashed with images, palimpsest and ever-rotating, none staying for more than a few seconds: a priest held out his hand to a prostrate crowd; a mass of movement, slowly revealed to be a huge flock of dark-winged birds; a series of lights and colors, the same abstract pattern three times in a row; a figure leaping from a skyscraper only to be cradled by a giant net. On they came, like those nightmare digital flashcards my father swore would improve my memory. A migraine built behind my left eye.

Slowly, I adjusted to the darkness.

Around the globe were chairs, each with straps on the arm, biker helmets above them. Probably forty of them, in concentric circles, facing the projection. What in the—

A figure in one of the chairs. A person. I jumped backwards, but they didn't move. A brighter-than-usual flash on the globe illuminated their opaque helmet, wrists bound by ropes to the armrests.

I rushed forward, fumbled at the ropes. They were covered in a bulky body suit and a feeding tube dangled from an empty bag beside them. The helmet concealed their whole head, wires connecting it to a box on the back of the chair. I fought back the urge to vomit. So this was how they were conditioning the clones. I knew what I'd find when I lifted the helmet away, and I was glad I'd left Theo behind. No one should have to witness their sibling in such a nightmarish condition.

I unbound their hands, wondering if this clone would try to kill me on sight but unable to leave them imprisoned. Braced myself and pulled off the helmet.

Kay stared back at me, eyes wide and blood-shot.

"Dora?" she asked, as though I were a ghost. Or she was. Blood spotted on her cracked lips. It was her, I was certain, the look in her eyes proof enough. Even so, I asked.

"Tell me." My voice like ice shattering. "If it's really you, tell me something only you'd know." I tried to think. "Like . . . the tattoo design I sketched for you." It had been on her corkboard when I left. No idea how long she'd waited to remove it, hours or years.

She made a sound that should have been a laugh and lifted one too-thin arm. "I had it done," she said. "That bloody, triumphant fist."

I clutched her to me. "I thought you were dead, Kay. I thought . . . We'll get you out of here." She was shaking under me, and I thought I could feel the rapid beat of her heart through the room's incessant whispers.

Then everything went silent. The projections ceased and lights came up.

"Well, Theodore, this is hardly the homecoming I envisioned."

I knew the voice before I looked up, before I saw him, flanked on one side by a guard in a rumpled uniform and on the other by a clone with Theo's face and a bushy mustache. In the decade since

I'd last seen the man they escorted, his face had changed. He still had the nose I'd inherited, the too-thin lips, but his deep black hair was silver now, and his pockmarked features had, infuriatingly, aged gracefully. But he seemed smaller, diminished, his hands balled into fists, even as his face was lit with triumph.

Both of his minions had guns drawn, my clone with what looked like another 9mm, the security guard with a mag-propulsion weapon. The kind that had killed Valk. Kay's back was to them, her chair between us and the trio. Not that it mattered. A mag-propelled round might well rip through the chairback, Kay, and me and keep going. I let go of Kay, trying not to glance to my .38 where I'd left it on the chair next to her.

"I should have known it was you, Trevor," I said, ignoring his deadname bait.

"My friends call me Trevor," he said. "If you won't call me 'Father,' then 'Dr. Madsen' will suffice." He seemed almost perfectly calm. That was when he was most dangerous, when he was harnessing his rage, channeling it. I had to keep him talking. My only chance. *Kay's* only chance.

"How'd you get my DNA?" Seemed like the place to start. Clone and guard kept their weapons aimed at me, center mass. I'd be dead before I could raise my gun.

"Oh, Theodore," he said. "Of course I had contingencies. I've been protecting you from yourself since you were in diapers."

"Is that what you call trying to murder me?"

"You murdered my son long ago." He ran his hand through gelled-back hair. "It just took me a while to see it."

"So you're, what? Growing a better version of me?" I failed to keep my voice steady. I was going to die here, but maybe I could make a difference for Kay. For the commune. Maybe I could still put something right.

"So shortsighted," Madsen said. "As always. This isn't about you. It's not even about clones." He scoffed. "As though money won't buy you racks of organ-replacement vessels off-shore? My employer didn't invest all these resources in something as trivial as *cloning*. The clones are the canvas. Behavioral Cybernetics is the masterpiece. It will change the world."

"This is all about *behavior modification*?" The holy grail of authoritarians the world over. Far as I could see, they already had most of the power. But one thing you can count on with people like

Madsen: they always want more.

"You've always lacked vision, Theodore." He slipped comfortably into his lecturing tone. As close as I'd ever seen him to happy, except when he was lost in his research. "I'm talking about utopia. A better, happier society. Social cohesion. Unity. Real reform of criminals. An end to mental illness."

"Complaint workers," I spat. "Conversion therapy. The end of resistance. Of difference. A fist crushing a human throat, forever."

His smile like a crocodile's. "I failed you, Theodore. I can admit that. Your mother had her own ideas, and I didn't understand the damage she was doing. We—"

"Don't you fucking talk about her!" I screamed.

"I made mistakes with you," he continued serenely. "And my techniques weren't advanced enough to fix you, not back then. And now it's too late—"

The lights switched off. Complete darkness. I scrambled for the .38, my grip closing around its reassuring bulk. Dropped prone. Emergency lights came up, their red eyes unblinking.

"Green," Madsen said to the clone. "Get to Ops, right now. Get the power back up." The clone departed. No way I was a better shot than the guard, but—

"You will slide your gun to me, son." Madsen's voice held no hint of emotion. "Or Mr. Lee here will put three rounds through your friend."

Kay groaned. "Don't, Dora . . ." I didn't need her to finish the thought. If I gave up the gun, we were both dead. Or worse. I needed a shot, but the guard had stepped to one side, where a pillar provided him with cover. His shot at Kay was easy, my shot at him, hopeless.

The thought of Kay dead before me. Again. There are limits. Steps your legs refuse to take, necessity be damned.

I slid the gun across the floor.

"That's good," Madsen said, with a perfect, triumphant smile. "Now, I'll give you a choice—"

The click of a hammer being drawn back. Theo, behind the guard, the pistol's chrome like a sharp tongue in the dark. I wondered briefly if Madsen was proud to finally have a child who learned quickly.

"Drop the weapon," Theo hissed at the guard. Lee set it down, slow, eyes on his boss the whole time.

"Oh, Blue." Madsen shook his head. "He's got

you all twisted up. Look at yourself. Putting a gun on Lee, who's never done anything to you. Helping this traitor."

Theo's spine snapped taut at that last word, eyes flicking between us. That would be the programming kicking in. Fuck. I inched forward. My revolver maybe ten feet away. If Theo turned against me, I'd never get there.

"Stop. Talking." Theo's jaw clenched, eyes wide and dark.

"Think about this reasonably," Madsen said like he wasn't at risk having his brains blown out. "It's like I warned you. Out there, things can mess you up. Get everything twisted. You've been feeling lost, haven't you? Confused. I can see it in your eyes."

Fucking hell. I didn't know shit about shit, but I could see the warped foundation Madsen had laid.

"You don't need to do what he says, Theo," I said.

"Oh, he's right, you know," Madsen replied. "You don't need to. I'm glad you picked that name, Blue. Excuse me, Theodore. You could be him, you know. My true son. It's there for the taking. You just need to trust me."

"Trust him to control you. To make you into

a weapon again!" I edged forward a few more inches. Theo's hand wavering, the lights making blood of the sweat running down that familiar forehead. Soon it would run into Theo's eyes and burn, just as it always did with mine.

"A simple choice," Madsen said, his voice never rising. "Give yourself over to his confusion, to his decadence, or come." He lifted an open palm. "And be my son."

Theo hesitated, gun-hand dropping slightly. Like a fool, I'd thought a few days could undo all that trauma, all that twisting up, all the ways they'd rewired his neurons.

"He couldn't even make *me* his son, Theo." I hated the barely restrained sob in my voice. "He can't make you anyone you don't want to be." Didn't know if that was true, but all I had left was the hope it might be.

Theo's face was warped by agony, an expression like cornered prey. Theo screamed like someone dying, and raised the gun over the guard's shoulder, muzzle pointed at Madsen.

The guard grabbed Theo's arm. I threw myself forward, scrambling across the floor, reaching for the .38. Madsen did the same. He was closer. But I knew what it was to fight or die.

Grunts and sharp breaths. All of us dark shadows. My fingers closed over the revolver's grip. Madsen arrived a fraction later, grabbed at it. I yanked it away, smashed the butt across his face. Pain like heat-lightning lancing from my broken fingers up my arm.

Madsen staggered back, fell to the ground. A shot echoed. My ears rang, my revolver still cold, I turned—

Theo was on the ground, oil-black liquid welling from my clone's gut. The guard held Theo's 9mm. Just like with Valk, the first shot had been center mass. One more piece clicked into place, utterly indifferent to its terrible timing. I didn't know how they'd figured out Valk was behind Kay's—clone Kay's—death, but they'd sent Lee, or someone who might as well have been Lee, to tie up that loose end. At the commune, I'd seen Lee's work. Just like with Valk, he'd put another round in Theo's gut, then one in the head.

Someone shouted. Maybe me, or Theo, or Kay, or all of us. My first shot caught the guard in the shoulder. He staggered. The second took him in the chest. He hit the pillar hard, slumped down. A bubble on his lips like he was chewing gum. Even now he tried to raise his weapon. I put a round between his eyes.

In the light, there'd be blood and tissue everywhere. In this hellpit, only a dark well where Lee's face used to be.

I staggered, fighting for breath, almost tripped over Theo, whose hands clutched the wound, gleaming wet. A gut shot, probably didn't hit the spine. Theo might be okay, might be—

A sound behind me. I whirled. Only Kay, stumbling forward, falling to Theo's side. Madsen was on all fours, a yard from the mag weapon.

"Give me a reason," I said, and Madsen stopped like I'd punched him, sagged to the ground. I grabbed the gun, went to Theo.

Kay was trying to put pressure on the wound but could barely keep herself upright. I ripped off my jacket, pressed it down on the where the blood was welling.

"Where's your first aid kit?" I shouted at Madsen. No answer. Theo's eyes unfocused, mouth lolling. I'd asked Theo to stay behind. *Told* Theo to stay behind. My clone's shuddering breath. My shuddering breath. The guns on the ground beside me. Theo needed the pressure. And first aid. Kay too weak. Madsen silent.

"I'll shoot you if you don't tell me," I said.

"You will anyway," Madsen said. He was afraid, but not panicked.

I was usually cool under pressure, but now that was failing me. Killing Madsen wouldn't save Theo. Same with not killing him.

"Breathe," I told Theo and myself. "Breathe. You'll be okay." Theo's mouth opened. Maybe trying to speak. I leaned down. Rasping breath against my ear. My hands and Kay's pressing down, sticky-wet.

The lights came up. Everywhere desperate faces, blood and viscera on concrete.

"You never lacked for tenacity, Theodore," Madsen said, smirking like I couldn't end him. Green was coming back, probably with others. I should take a defensive position. We were all dead if I let them get the jump on us.

My hands stayed where they were, kept the pressure on Theo's wound.

"No clever rejoinder?" Madsen said. Dead Gods, I wanted him to die.

The door swung open. I braced myself.

Juan and Lylah stood in the doorway. A sight almost as shocking as finding Kay alive.

"Oh fuck," Juan said.

"Kay?" Lylah asked.

Juan rushed forward, into the carnage. Lylah stood frozen in the doorway, caught between hope and terror. I knew the feeling.

"Help," I said, my tongue thick. "Juan, please."

He was unlatching something. A first aid kit. I couldn't make sense of what was happening.

"Blue told us your plan," Juan said, not looking at me. Setting to work. All business. "Thought you could use a hand."

"Theo," I said, stupidly. "Blue's name is Theo."

Juan nodded, didn't stop moving. "Lylah, I need help."

Lylah stood, eyes locked with Kay's. Whatever I was feeling, it had to wait. Lylah must have felt the same. She rushed forward to assist.

"You can let go, Dora," Juan said. My hands weren't responding. "I'll handle this. Keep us safe."

A double kindness, far more than I deserved. I checked the safety on the mag weapon, went to put it in my jacket pocket, forgetting it was being peeled from Theo's abdomen. Tucked it in the back of my jeans instead. Grabbed the 9mm from beside Lee's body. No way for Madsen to get at it. I had a few moments to decide.

Whatever Madsen saw in my face shattered his

calm. He pushed himself away from me, pressed his back to a pillar. His gaze went to Lee, and I had the pleasure of watching him rethink his location when it was too late.

Not as much pleasure as I'd expected. Valk was dead, Kay—who even knew? Red, who'd only done what he'd been made to do. And Theo—there was so much blood.

Madsen's eyes met mine, then trailed to my gun.

"I'm unarmed," he said. "Not a threat." True and false. But not an immediate one.

"Look at what you've done," I demanded, my free hand gesturing behind me. "Because I wouldn't be who you wanted."

"Look at where your defiance has led you, Theodore," he said. He stared past me, at my friends. My former friends.

"Leaving home was the best decision I ever made," I said. Thought for a moment. "Second best. My name's Dora."

He opened his mouth, closed it again. No matter how tough he liked to seem, he didn't want to catch a bullet over my deadname. Hard, suddenly, not to see him as small, a man so desperate for control that he'd iterate versions of me to get the one he wanted. I felt my resolve twist and break. Even now, even with him, I couldn't bring myself to do it. If only he were armed . . .

He must have seen it in my eyes. He relaxed fractionally. As I always did when I couldn't make sense of my emotions, I pivoted to intellect.

"Give me answers," I said, "and maybe I'll let you walk out of here."

He scoffed, but I knew him well. Whether he lived or died, he'd want to demonstrate his superiority.

"Your employer couldn't risk being caught with a cloning operation," I speculated. Keeping their name out of things. Never knew who might be listening. "So they set this up for you. Cleared out the neighborhood to make sure no one was around to notice clones. Maybe you were even planning to found your own community, once things were far enough along."

He grinned. Despite everything, flashed a Godsdamned shit-eating grin. "Very good, Th—" His eyes snapped to my gun, and he stopped himself. "Very good. First, we'd prove that the system worked for individuals. Then we'd show what it could do in a neighborhood."

One of the worst failure modes of commune

was cult. The room smelled of blood and shit. Bile flooded my mouth. "And you used my DNA because you had it handy," I said. "And because you wanted to prove you could make a 'better' version of me."

"A perfected version," he said.

I ignored the provocation. "But why clone Kay?"

He kept his smirk under control. Barely. "My employers couldn't bribe your friends. And once corporate intel's background check told me they knew you, I needed them cleared out."

I followed a tickle at the back of my brain, my intuition whispering to me. Better that than thinking of Theo possibly dying behind me. "But Bi—but the corporation—didn't want to risk drawing attention by eliminating the commune."

He laughed. "Don't ask me why. Nobody cared about a bunch of squatters, dealers, addicts in this neighborhood. They wouldn't care about your friends playing utopia, either. But, yes, they refused.

"So I took matters into my own hands. The hardest part was the abduction. But Kay was a user, you see. Went out into the neighborhood alone. Terribly dangerous, really. Then I just needed to wait for the cloning and conditioning."

Kay'd been quiet recently, Samara had told me.

"How long?" I asked, trembling.

He tilted his head in what I'd always thought of as his recollection pose. "Six weeks, three days. It was perfect, until that bitch fucked it up. I knew she'd been talking to the competition, but didn't expect her to be so . . . murderous."

"And you killed her to make sure she'd not tell what she knew."

"Look at what you're capable of, even now. If you'd been my good son, this triumph would be ours to share."

I took a deep breath. Never killed anyone who wasn't an active threat. Madsen wasn't worth breaking that code for, I told myself. Even so, it was a struggle.

"You don't want to know what I'm capable of—"

A noise from outside. I stumbled to the doorway, peeked out, expecting to see Green coming back with more guards. What I saw was much worse.

Five figures advanced down the hallway. I knew none of them. Four had the same uniform Lee wore, but carefully pressed. They carried mag rifles, each worth more than I'd ever seen in one place. They surrounded the fifth, who wore a hard femme skirt suit and real silk top. Their skin was a bit darker than mine, their hair buzzed save for one long, slick wave cascading down their right side. High-end tech, integrated into their skin, ran up their arms and disappeared under the suit coat. I pulled back into the room.

The others had cut Theo's shirt away, packed gauze onto the wound. My clone was still breathing, but no way ready to be moved. And our only exit was blocked by corporate firepower.

"We've got company coming," I said. All eyes on me. I tucked away my .38. "Keep working. No sudden moves. I'll talk them down."

I glanced at Madsen, expecting the smirk to return, but he'd gone very pale.

When they came through the door, I was standing between them and my friends, palms up. The others all huddled over Theo.

"I wondered when Corporate would show up," I said, hoping I sounded confident. The scene behind me didn't help.

The guards fanned out, weapons not quite pointed at any of us.

Skirt Suit raised a perfectly shaped eyebrow. "You're not a clone."

"No," I said, hands still in the air. Theo's blood matted on my palms. "I'm the blueprint. My name's Dora."

Their eyes flicked from me to Madsen. "I see the resemblance," they said. They weren't armed, that I could see, but a word from them would end us all. "You may call me Case."

I only had one play. Long odds, but better than none. "I assume you didn't sign off on Madsen using clones as hit persons?"

Case's eyes studied Madsen. Another raised eyebrow.

"No need for hysterics," Madsen said. "It was a necessary test to establish limits of control, and he was a potential problem—"

"More than a potential one, it seems," Case said casually. The look in their eyes was calculating, emotionless. A perfect corporate operative, weighing everything as entries on a spreadsheet.

"Only because he came after me." I gestured to the others. "After us. Replacing us with clones."

Madsen's expression fell further. He masked it quickly, but not quick enough. I'd guessed correctly about how badly he'd overstepped. "That's absurd. *He's* just trying to talk his way out of where his choices have brought him."

He'd never understood me. Still didn't. I'd come into his lab expecting to die. This wasn't about talking my way out. Not for me, anyway. But I wanted better for my friends. For Lylah, even. For Theo, whatever we were to each other. For Kay.

Kay. "My friend here," I said. "She's a member of the commune. And he's got clones of her growing in the other room."

Case didn't give much away, but I could tell that information didn't surprise them. They'd already seen Kay's clones.

Madsen was ready for that one. "Just another subject to test on," he said. "Nothing more."

Just like that, I knew how to stop him. To make sure he couldn't harm anyone ever again. Not pulling the trigger, quite, but without any moral difference. All I had to do was break another of my rules. Funny, how things that seem to matter deeply for so long can become suddenly inconsequential. I hesitated only a moment before I condemned him.

"I have memory implants." For a moment, I felt I was looking down at myself from above, my voice cool, unconcerned. Like I hadn't sworn to myself to keep my memories private. Like I didn't know lives hinged on what I said. "Would you like to see the proof for yourself, Case?"

There it was. Panic in Madsen's eyes. Don't know that I'll ever have closure, but it was quite satisfying.

"He's—he's fucking with you, Case!" Madsen shouted. "You need me—"

"I don't think that will be necessary, Dora," Case said, and gave the slightest nod to one of her goons, who raised their rifle and, *pft pft*, put two rounds into Madsen's head. The shots no louder than a paintball gun's. Madsen wheezed a single breath. Then silence. I stared at what was left of my father.

Someone else had killed him, but I'd as good as ordered it. There was a certain symmetry in that: he'd ordered others killed, ordered me killed. Now he was finished. I'd get the shakes, the nausea, later. Relief came first. But I couldn't savor it, couldn't trust it. Not yet.

"We certainly did not authorize Dr. Madsen's actions, Dora." Case said. Hard to read their face, but I'd have bet anything they were calculating relative costs of eliminating witnesses.

"I figured he was a rogue agent," I said, walking a tightrope I couldn't clearly see. What would they want, and what could I offer? More than anything, they needed not to be tied to what happened here. Heat from other corps, trouble with local law. We only mattered to them to the extent we affected their cost/benefit calculations.

"Indeed," Case said. "This entire operation was unauthorized." Clearly a lie, but best for both of us if I believed it.

"They just want to keep living in the neighborhood as always," I said, gesturing behind me. "Don't have any beef with—" I stopped myself. "With whoever's paying your bills." Sweat trickled down my back. Easy to imagine them killing us here, not much harder to see them wiping out the commune.

Case glanced at the others, then back at me. One manicured nail tapped against their chin. "My employers would be disappointed if anyone was slandering them as a result of a rogue contractor."

Another careful line to walk. "Even if we knew who employed you, we aren't narcs," I said, but that was commune language. I switched approaches. "And there's nothing in it for us." I stifled the urge to say more. Let them come to their own conclusions. That there were others who knew about us, enough that disappearances might draw questions.

They'd rejected this as too risky before. And who cared what a bunch of squatters said? Who would we even tell?

Hard not to blurt out all that, but Case, corporate prick or not, was no fool. Don't protest too much.

"I see that," Case said, and looked to the others. "Is your friend telling the truth?"

"Yes. We just want this behind us," Kay said. Lylah's arms around her. Theo pale on the floor.

"Very well," Case said. "Be on your way, then. Leave the clone." She gestured, almost casually, to where Theo was bleeding out.

I felt us all tense as one.

"That's not going to happen," Juan said. He leaned over Theo, didn't look back. Kept at his work.

"Oh?" Case's tone twisted my guts.

"You can shoot us," Lylah said, her fingers clenched against Kay's shoulder. "But we're not going to let you hurt Theo."

One guard's finger twitched. Not much, but enough. We were fucked.

"Leave my twin out of this." I was reacting, not thinking. "They've got nothing to do with my— with Madsen's folly here."

A long pause. Case sizing me up. Calling Theo

my twin was another fiction between us, but only barely. I held my breath, willed them to not bother with us.

"Very well. You're trespassing on private property. Get out."

We used a plywood frame from one of the bunks to move Theo, still far too risky, but better than watching an execution.

"Dora," Case said lightly, just as we were about to hoist Theo up. I turned. The operative looked like someone who only sweat if they chose to. "You know what happens if any of this comes back on my employers." A threat, but delivered as professional courtesy.

"It won't," I said, held their gaze. They nodded. We picked up Theo, turned our backs on them. No gunfire, no *pft* of mag propulsion. We were clear.

Slept the next day in my bathroom, and pretty well, given the throb of my fingers and the way every sound felt like an ambush. Met up with Smith that night.

"They've cleared out," I said, trying to read those glowing eyes, having little luck. "BioGesis. The head of their operation here had Valk killed. And then they killed him for overstepping."

Not even a raised eyebrow, Smith's face flatter than flat. "You're sure?"

"I watched them do it. You can confirm they've shut down, if you like." I told him how to find the place. EvoTech would be hours too late to get anything useful, but there should be enough traces to confirm my story.

"What were they doing?" he asked. I wondered how much he knew. Impossible to say.

"Something involving behavioral development of full clones." A premonition stretched before me, everyone working to scratch itches they couldn't name, itches some corp development team implanted. More of the same, just worse. "Didn't work out. The clones turned on their masters."

Smith tilted his head, considering. Evaluating. Even with a few hours' sleep, exhaustion meant it was all I could do to keep my hands steady. It's one reason I wasn't lying: I'd be caught. There was another reason. "They know they were discovered, but you're still alive."

A challenge. Just like Case, Smith would kill

me if he thought it worthwhile. Well. I could catch a bullet now, if that's how it had to be.

"I think they decided I wasn't worth disappearing. I don't have any proof, after all. And they know I'm not about to go to the cops."

"Well," Smith said. "Assuming this all checks out . . ." He paused. This is where I was supposed to say *it will*. I don't like scripts. When I didn't budge, he continued. "Then you've done your part. Solved a riddle for my employer. Set back BioGesis's plans."

I waited.

"Assuming you sign the NDA, I can get you paid for this," Smith went on. No doubt they had a budget for such things. I wondered how little it cost EvoTech to buy whatever words or silences they needed.

"I'll sign," I said. "On one condition."

The hint of a frown on Smith's face.

"Valk's mother. She still needs her medication. That deal must be honored."

To my surprise, the operative smiled. "Yes," he said. "It does."

We worked out the details quickly. I didn't bother to threaten. It would be pointless. What's a lifetime of doses for one elder? For my community, a nearly incomprehensible boon. For EvoTech? Near enough to nothing.

Smith made it a handful of steps before turning around. "Dora," he said. "If you're ever looking for work, my employer could use your skill set."

"I don't work corporate," I told him.

"I know," Smith said. "But you might be available for contract work?"

I almost refused. But this case had cost me almost every cent I had, and keeping that channel open might matter down the line.

"You know how to reach me," I said.

A week later, and I was still waking up convinced someone was in my apartment, or screaming as too-vivid faces of the dead rose from the cauldron of my dreams. I'd had worse, and for less reason. Worst part was waiting for word on Theo. I couldn't get my clone out of my thoughts, couldn't escape the terror that Theo would die without even a thank-you from me.

I needed work but couldn't focus enough to

look for it. Didn't do anything but sleep and wake and agonize. At least the itching in my fingers backed off some.

Word came at last, from a new burner number: "It's T. They tell me my scar will be cool. Stop by? I don't know your security protocols, sorry."

The commune guards nodded to me, not a hint of a frown. Inside, two adolescents coordinated a group of kids repainting a wall in vivid colors. A warm smell brought me up short. Someone was baking honest-to-Gods bread in the kitchen. Kay and Juan rose from a table to greet me. Kay, braced on a cane, was still pale. But a marked improvement.

"You're looking good," I said, meaning it and knowing how cruel I'd been to her. Shoved my hands in my pockets.

"You too, Dora," Kay said. Her face was open as ever, like I'd never severed myself from the community, never hurt her to ease my own pain, never left behind the life we'd all been building. She pulled me into a hug, kissed my cheek.

Juan hugged me, too. "You did just like you said, Dora," he told me. "You solved it."

"And you saved my life," I said.

"Only because Theo told us what was up," he

said. "You really don't have to take on everything alone, Dora." His tone so gentle I couldn't resent it.

"Theo's upstairs," Kay added.

I'd foolishly imagined Theo in my old room, but Theo's was down the corridor. My clone was propped on the mattress, enjoying a bowl of something warm. Samuel kept watch. When I entered, he smiled.

"Good to see you, Dora." Samuel hugged me. "I'll give you two some time."

I took a seat. Theo and I stared anywhere but at each other.

"Well," my clone said, "they tell me I didn't imagine it. You really talked some bigwig out of shooting me."

"Did what I could," I said.

"Saved my life," Theo insisted.

"Well," I said. "It's only fair. You saved mine."

"Only after trying to kill you." Theo's smile dropped away.

"They—he—programmed you to be a murderer," I said. "And look what you are instead."

I watched Theo consider that. "It doesn't feel that way," Theo said. "But maybe it will someday."

I'd been feeling the same way. "So, what's next for you? Once you're healed up?" I asked into lingering silence.

"I'm going to stay here," Theo said. Joy and longing twisted like a storm front in my gut. "I have a lot of knots to untangle, and this is where I want to do that."

"I'm glad," I said. "You'll fit in well here."

Theo's mouth opened and closed. Gave up on one thought, tried another. "Have you considered . . . Dora, is it possible you're a clone, too?"

I'd thought about that. My memory problems could be a symptom of high-level fucking with my brain. But they could also be a sign of more typical trauma, like being a trans kid with a father who hates you. "I don't think so," I said. "But I can't rule it out. If he didn't want me to know . . ." I took a deep breath. "Dissociation is rough, and it can chew up your memory. But sometimes . . . sometimes it kept me alive." Not really an answer, but all I could say for sure.

"I'm so sorry, Dora." Theo's voice dropped almost to a whisper. "Would it be bad if you were a clone?"

"No! Not at all. There's nothing special about whoever is the original." That much I was certain of. "Don't ever let anyone tell you where you came from is who you are."

Some of the tension went out of Theo's shoulders. "Then what you said, Dora, to that corporate lady. About me being your twin . . ."

I felt my ears burning. "I needed a lie," I said. "If I admitted you were one of the clones . . ."

Theo nodded. "Yeah. That makes sense." This was the part where we had a serious conversation about what we were to one another, and how we felt about that.

Maybe if I'd been someone else. We sat in not-super-comfortable silence.

"I should let you rest," I managed at last.

"Will I see you around?" my clone asked.

"Yeah," I said. "If you want to. I mean, I'd like that." And me still with even less idea who Theo was to me than who Kay was.

"Good. That's good."

I stood, unsure where to put my hands, where to look.

"Well," Theo added. "It was good to work with you, Dora. And to answer your question, I think they/them pronouns suit me best. At least for the moment."

"Thanks." I felt my smile stretch wide. "For sharing that with me, Theo. And . . . and for saving me."

Kay and Juan were waiting for me down be-low. Lylah and Samara had joined them. Even Lylah wasn't glowering, though her arm tightened around Kay's waist when she saw me. Possessive, but I couldn't blame her. I wouldn't trust me, either.

Bread was on the table, a whole loaf, an un-imaginable bounty.

"Join us?" Samara asked, all smiles. Strange to have been more comfortable with worry, distrust. I sat, and Kay split off big chunks of bread, dark brown and steaming. Handed me one.

"I shouldn't," I said. "This is commune food."

"Please," Kay said. "Don't decline. It's offered freely, and in friendship."

For the first time since my return, I saw a hint of worry on their faces. Like they thought I'd fallen so far that I expected a shared meal to be transactional. Maybe they were right.

I took a bite. So hot it almost burned, a crisp edge and soft inside. I chewed slowly. The others did the same. So easy, coming back to this.

A thick porridge followed the bread. Not as good, but far better than I'd eaten in months. Could barely taste the protein mash beneath real fresh vegetables from the garden. Chatter about commune business, a planned tribute to Valk, friendly gossip about a recently formed triad, three younger members of the commune who were cloying in their affections. No effort to conceal any of this from me. I knew what was coming, even as I struggled to believe it.

"You did this community a great service, Dora," Juan said at last. "Even after we kicked you out. You saved us."

I shook my head. "We saved each other."

Glances among the group, then a series of nods.

"Yes," Lylah said. A smile, despite the tension in her jaw. "But the point is, the commune has talked about it, and there's consensus. Anyone who'd do what you did for us is welcome here."

A flash of annoyance on Juan's face. He'd not wanted Lylah to deliver the message.

"Ly's right, Dora," Kay said, leaning against her girlfriend. "You have a home here. If you want."

I did want it. Desperately. I just hadn't let myself realize it until right then. I could see it so clearly, working in the garden again, bickering over every small thing, laughing and singing in the evenings, sweating and bleeding together. Lylah and I low-key hating each other for no good reason. Watching Theo become themself . . .

Theo, who was ready. Theo, who was open, seeking.

And me? I felt the potential failure like stitches bursting. I'd join the security committee again, push for what I thought were obvious changes. In the ragged depths of my heart, I was still the girl afraid to lose what little she had, to lose anyone else she loved. I'd hold on too tight. Pick fights again, lose the arguments again. I'd fuck up like I'd done before. I was my father's daughter, at least in that way. Clinging to my friends like I owned them. Mistaking control for protection. For love.

I'd been willing to destroy the commune to keep it safe. I'd refused Theo's help, like I had any right to make that choice for him. What would I do the next time we faced an existential threat? And there's always a next time.

Truth was, I didn't know what I'd do. Until I did, I couldn't trust myself. Couldn't ask anyone else to trust me, either.

"I can't," I said. Shock in every face. Except Juan's. "Not yet. I have—I have to sort some things out, or I'll be a problem again."

"I wanted you to stay last time, too," Kay said, very softly.

"I know. And I should have. But now . . ." I didn't know how to say it. But I felt the truth, like rocks sewn into my stomach.

"When you're ready, then," Samara said. Tears in her eyes. I had to look away.

"And you'll come by and see us?" Kay's voice quavered. "I know Theo hopes you will. We do, too."

I could only nod. The wanting had its hooks in me, but that wasn't enough to fix anything. I pushed myself to my feet.

"I will," I said. "I promise. And—and if you ever need help . . ." No more words. What they needed from me, I wasn't able to give. Not yet.

Late afternoon when I left, and summer had broken at last. The cold air made my lungs ache. I pulled up my hood, walked alone through the silent neighborhood. No steam from the manholes, the crumbling buildings. Only my breath, clouding before me.

AFTERWORD

I'm suspicious of metaphor. Not that I don't like a good metaphor—far from it. But the idea that science fiction is, or should be, the fiction of literalized metaphors has never had much appeal to me. This isn't to say that such approaches have no value. Samuel R. Delaney observed that sentences such as "his world exploded" and "she turned on her left side" may mean something very different—and potentially very literal— in a science fictional context from what they'd mean in other genres. This is a valuable insight, not to be dismissed. But such literalization has its limits because the process of literalizing the metaphor also forecloses other possibilities for that metaphor. Once the linguistic ambiguity of "she turned on her left side" resolves itself, that metaphor becomes anchored to a fixed, literal meaning within the narrative. If it's a science fiction tale, once her left side powers up, its servos whir, its microchips process data, the metaphor's meaning is (more-or-less) fixed.

My own instincts run contrary to such literalization. I prefer my metaphors to explode in the same sense that the Big Bang was an explosion. I don't want metaphors that collapse into a fixed meaning. I want ones that expand in unpredictable ways.

These Fragile Graces, This Fugitive Heart started with the clones. More specifically, it started with the idea of a trans woman being pursued by her own clones. Clones have a long history in science fiction, and they're often read as doppelgängers or as a kind of mirror, even if it's a fun house mirror (as in the film *Us*), showing us an uncanny version of ourselves. But this conception is limited, in part because the overwhelming majority of people who have engaged with clones-as-metaphor are cisgender (that is, their gender identity matches the gender they were assigned at birth). But if you cloned me, a transgender woman, and if that clone didn't themself transition, they'd be in some ways precisely like me (after all, we'd share 100 percent of our DNA). But in other ways they couldn't be more different. If you put me face-to-face with my clone, my experience wouldn't be anything like looking into a mirror.

Nor would it be precisely like Samara and Samuel's experience, two identical twins with different genders, who have grown up with a combination of similarity and difference from one another that is related to and distinct from what Dora is experiencing.

What *would* be the experience of meeting my clone? That's one of the questions that drew me to this novella. But while I started with that question, it's not the one that came to haunt me. The question that haunts me is not "what is it like for a trans woman to meet her clone?" but rather its inverse: "what is that meeting like *for her clone*?"

I love Dora. I love her messiness, how she's flawed and problematic, how she's trying—and largely failing—to escape the damage of her childhood. I know her well. She doesn't surprise me. But Theo? Theo surprised me.

Theo was part of my plan for this novella from its earliest stages. Long before they—or Dora, for that matter—had a name, Theo was always going to be a presence because I wasn't interested in collapsing the clone metaphor(s). And because what I really wanted was for Dora and Theo to bounce off each other, to put pressure on each other's assumptions about the world, about family, and about themselves. Without Theo, and without Theo's insistence on being *themself*, the clone metaphor might have been more easily reduced. One might read the clones as (only) a challenge to Dora's sense of self, taking us back to the funhouse mirror. That version of *These Fragile Graces* would have been tidier, its metaphors made straightforward, its meaning more easily fixed. Dora would have still grappled with her sense of self, but in a way that is common for clones-as-metaphor. Possibilities would have narrowed. What might have been a metaphorical explosion would have collapsed back in on itself. (And if we collapse it far enough, a metaphor always breaks down until, like the event horizon of a black hole, there's no way to see beyond it. But that is a topic for another day.)

Theo exploded the metaphor, and they exploded it through the force of their desires. When they emerged as their own character, deeply traumatized and under the effects of brainwashing, they nevertheless found themself *wanting*, and wanting intensely. I didn't anticipate how desperately they'd cling to the commune, nor their bone-deep need to be useful (though I should have, since Dora shares it).

I certainly never guessed how thoroughly they would "catch feelings" for Dora.

Here's the part where you can psychoanalyze Theo, or Dora, or me as much as you like. I'm not going to stop you. What I will say is that I tried to write the story without Theo and Dora hooking up, and Theo wouldn't let me. Just like they wouldn't let Dora settle for easy answers. Suffering, high on adrenaline, and desperate for human connection, Theo wants what they want.

Dora argues against Theo's desires—and her own. Of course she does! She cares deeply about consent, and hasn't had time to think through what consent means for a clone of undetermined age. She makes what I think is a pretty good argument. But Theo surprises her, just as they surprised me. And the greatest surprise, the one that I see as the heart of the scene, is that Theo demands to be treated as Dora's equal. They demand, in other words, that Dora live her anarchist values, that she accept Theo as their own person with agency and a right to self-determination.

You might be saying: *still, this is kind of messed up.*

Yes, absolutely. And Dora and Theo deserve to be able to make messed-up choices. Some people, especially cisgender, heterosexual white men, have long been allowed to be problematic. We aren't really approaching anything like true equity and equality until trans characters, and characters of other marginalizations, get to be every bit as flawed, as messy, as *human* as everyone else.

Maybe that's why I'm so suspicious of literalized metaphor. I want fiction that explores the range of human experience, that engages with joy, yes, but also with the ways we fail ourselves and one another. My experience, and those of other trans people, aren't reducible to metaphor. Or, at the very least, they're not reducible to straight(for-ward) metaphor.

Someday you, too, may look in the mirror (or at your clone) and see a stranger looking back at you. I don't know what that will mean for you, and most likely you don't, either, and won't know until it happens. What I do know is that, as mar-ginalized people fight to exist, be heard, and be un-derstood, what our doppelgängers/mirror selves/ clones mean will vary, shift, and change.

Those meanings—just like the meaning of Dora's choices, and Theo's—aren't fixed points. They are something we continue to make, as readers and writers, as individuals and communities. As with the expansion of the universe, we can't know in what new ways these meanings will unfurl. I take comfort in that because we'll make those meanings, and discover them, together.

—April 2023
Topeka, KS

ACKNOWLEDGMENTS

We accomplish nothing alone. We need our communities, our friends, and our chosen families. This book, which I drafted during the depths of the pandemic, is testament to that. Whenever I thought of despairing and giving up, loved ones were there to keep me going, just as they helped me get through those horrible times in many other ways. It's a cliché to say that all we have is one another, but that doesn't make it any less true.

Thanks to my agent, Dorian Maffei, who believed in this book and has been an enthusiastic advocate for it and for me. I am blessed to work with her.

Thanks to my editor, Jaymee Goh, who offered keen insights, guidance, wisdom, and kindness and let me gush over her cat. This book is much richer for having been in her hands.

Thanks to everyone at Tachyon, including publisher Jacob Weisman, managing editor Jill Roberts, designer Elizabeth Story, and publicists Kasey Lansdale and Rick Klaw. Their expertise and labor transformed a manuscript into a book, and I'm forever grateful.

Thanks to my wonderful, supportive parents and my amazing siblings. I love you all!

Many wonderful readers shared wisdom as I wrote and revised (and revised and revised). I'm beyond grateful for the feedback of Gary Jackson, Iori Kusano, R. B. Lemberg, Bogi Takács, and Natalia Theodoridou on drafts of this book.

On this and other projects, Shweta Adhyam, Elly Bangs, Andrea Martinez Corbin, A. T. Greenblatt, Alexandra Manglis, Vina Jie-Min Prasad, Adam Shannon, and Emma Törzs have tolerated my anxieties, provided guidance and comfort, and let me bounce roughly six million questions and ideas off of them.

My beloved Team Eclipse (Clarion West 2017) has continued to be a source of support, wisdom, and joy and has helped me through many challenges, whether by talking through craft problems, sharing joys and sorrows, or putting up with my periodic meltdowns.

Being trans in a deeply transphobic society is exhausting, and my trans community has held me close/up/together more times than I can count. This book is in many ways a love letter to you all.

Thanks to my animal companions, who can't read, but whom I'm thanking anyway.

Most of all, thanks to my spouse, Nora E. Derrington, who gives me endless love and support, makes me a better writer and person, and tolerates my terrible jokes.

IZZY WASSERSTEIN

Izzy Wasserstein is a queer, transgender woman who writes fiction and poetry. She is the author of dozens of short stories, two poetry collections, and the short-story collection *All the Hometowns You Can't Stay Away From* (Neon Hemlock Press, 2022). She was born and raised in Kansas, received her BA in English from Washburn University, and earned her MFA in Creative Writing from the University of New Mexico.

Wasserstein currently teaches writing and literature at a public university. She loves books, comics, horror movies, and slowly running long distances. She wants to hear about your D&D character. Wasserstein shares a home with her spouse, Nora E. Derrington, and their animal companions. *These Fragile Graces, This Fugitive Heart* is her debut novella.